# Cifiscape Vol. II
## The Twin Cities

# Cifiscape Vol. II
## The Twin Cities

**Written by**
John Beckmann • Doug Donley
Brian D. Garrity • Jonathan Hansen
Max Hrabal • Erica Lindquist
Aron Christensen • Bob Lipski
Dale Newton • David Oppegaard
Aaron M. Wilson

**Edited by**
Chastity West • Kit Martin
Jeffrey Martin • Pat Edmonson
Hannah Byrns-Enoch
Crystal Boyd

*For Henry Martin, without whom,
literally, none of this would be possible.*

Published by Onyx Neon Press, United States

ISBN-13 978-0-9779201-8-1

First Edition March, 2012

Cover Art by Jeffrey Martin

Designed and Typeset by Jeffrey Martin

**cifiscape.onyxneon.com**

# Index

# Introduction

*"That old saying, 'if it bleeds it leads,' is very true. Given all our devices which are binging all of the negative news to us 7 days a week, its no wonder we are pessimistic. Its no wonder people think the world is getting worse. But perhaps, that's not the case."*
Peter Diamandis 2012
X Prize Foundation

Hope. My father, Henry Martin, was a dreamer. His designs were wide ranging, but always focused on the practicality of getting to a solution. We need solutions today, when faced with what we have ahead, I wish I had thousand more of my father. But he died of heart complications right before the Christmas of 2009. I may be biased, because I'm in my twenties, and haven't seen as much as some, but from my perspective we are in a crisis. What has been before is passing away, and a new system should be put in place. We are faced with the end of the industrial age, and with it the high paying secure jobs that a production based economy brought along with it. We see around us a major skew towards services, and the mercurial insecurity of a thirty-nine hour a week, no benefits job that system provides. Our way of life consumes more than it produces, and whether we like it or not, it functions on borrowed money and resources, which basically equates to eating all the cake before feeding the baby. But it does not have to be this way.

I refuse to see change and lament what was. If we want the best possible future, we have to share a vision of what it will look like. Who we will be in this future is partly determined by what we say to each other. By not reinforcing negative distortions. When our ancestors sat around the fire and told stories about what lay beyond the ring of light, they could speak of monsters or angels. In the darkness beyond, we must use our imaginations to illuminate the leaves of the trees we cannot see. Those imaginations, however, can be bound by the ways of life we have seen before in the light of the day. The lives we have experienced in the past, the sight of oaks in the light, can, and should, inform our narratives of the forest at night.

When walking in a forest, there are well-hewn paths

cut through the undergrowth by generations of hikers. They have an assured beginning and an assured end. The feet of those that came before already mark the way. Their efforts make our walk comfortable and rapid. No vines entangle our feet. If the path doesn't go to our destination, if we need to get somewhere else, however, then the only thing to do is leave the trail, and set off in a new direction. The going is not as easy. We have to set our own destination, and clear the way for those who will come after us. We find ourselves needing a new course, to set a direction we need to discuss our goals.

I conceived Cifiscape during the spring of 2010. Though the name came about later, it encapsulates the idea: local authors narrating cities' futures. Simply put, we showcase local authors to build a shared narrative about where we are headed. These visions are not like the mythologies of the pioneers after they conquered the west, with all of the destroyed lives that movement caused, but about the daily lives of people in our world, trying to get somewhere new, with all of the struggle that entails.

In 2010 when I thought to accumulate new visions, the economy was in the dumps. I was working as a home loan officer, at that time, foreclosing on dozens of homes everyday. Our foreclosure operations expanded 10 fold during the few months I worked there. Throughout, I found inspiration in TED.com videos and realized a great deal is possible, if you get people working together. As Peter Diamandis' singularity university advocates, we need to democratize the power to change the world.

2010 was also a year of grieving for me. My father had passed away. My strongest memories of him are our night-time walks. We designed and built in our dreams: rocket ships, space elevators, zero-gravity gardens, solar powered futures, in short the dreams of the 1960's were still alive and well when my dad and I went for a walk. But on top of that we cooked up ways to implement the hydrogen car industry, the solar power industry, and increase literacy in Sudan with cell phones. I believe if he had lived, he would have changed the world. Though he would not agree with everything I will say here, that is the point, we have to include alternative ways of seeing the future, to get on a new course. The democratized inclusive voice needs to speak.

From this place in my life, weighed down by my economic situation, and wishing to dream like my father did, I put out a letter to local writing groups asking a simple question, "What do you think the future of Twin Cities will be like?" And authors let me know. I received graphic arts, and the beginnings of novels. I read the authors dreams with enthusiasm. I was going on those walks again. Pulling together my literary colleagues,  and my brother, Jeffrey we got the book published with Onyx Neon Press. We used a crowd sourced editing model to maximize participation in these dreams. And though — as Jeffrey always says — the crowd sourcing was highly chaotic. Amidst the chaos of Cifiscape Vol. I we found a great number of challenges, but by working together we also found success.

We found ourselves in new territory, bringing in new authors and crowd sourcing the editing process. On some days it felt like utter chaos. Yet, the chaos of working together without a well-worn way needs to be dwelled on. As you will see in the pages that follow, none of us, and I would imagine none of you, have all the answers. Democracy does not speak with a single voice. We did not get where we are because anyone knew the answers in the past either. Instead we got here by each of our progenitors working every day to take a whack at the problems of their time. My Uncle Steve, who was a criminal defense lawyer, told me one time, when I asked him how he could defend criminals taught me an important point: to keep the system just, someone has to defend the accused. Unless we work every day even a good situation can sour. Unless we share our hopes, dreams and fears we are going to end up in a sour situation.

That is why this logger jam in Washington, and Minnesota, between the US's two parties is so frustrating. While the parties fight, employment stays flat. While the parties fight, same sex discrimination continues in our laws and society. While the parties fight, children who were born in this country do not get access to education, because of the crimes of mothers and of fathers: crossing a border for a better life. Though both republicans and democrats have sought to reform immigration, the grid-lock is simply too tight. If we cannot get off this well-worn path through this forest with a vision of a future that leads in a new direction, we will exhaust our energy reserves as we walk back and forth. We will become a less inclusive society. We lose our children's future as we diverge into our camps.

For what? Short term gains. As Bill Clinton put it in *Back to Work*, we need to get back in the future business. Underlying Volume II is the idea that 'we need to hang together, or we will hang apart.' In short this anthology says *we should not build an exclusive society out of fear of losing what we have*. We see this through the narrative of our authors:

• **Choice:** Aaron M. Wilson's three-part parable, where America falls apart and Canadian socialism is an unbelievable dream, we splinter into cannibalism as we each become our own societies, with our own directions the idea of separation becomes clear.

• **Danger:** It is also apparent in Brian D. Garrity's take over by the outside, perhaps a satirical view of what a hostile takeover of the US would feel like when our debt becomes untenable.

• **Cooperation:** This notion that we must work together comes out in Doug Donley's character of Amos, his questions asks us to consider how our society would be, if we looked out for each other.

• **Realism**: We can't, however, simply dream of a better future. David Opppegard reminds us that a dream without reality ends lives.

• **Justice**: Erica Lindquist and Aron Christensen re-inforce the point that we need to stand up for ourselves, because otherwise, we may well be bullied.

• **Practicality**: Max Hrabal and Dale Newton re-mind us that the everyday actions to get by are still the most important.

• **Hope**: Bob Lipski shows us that betting on the future in this mess seems confusing.

• **Perseverance**: Jonathan Hansen recalls that even though this way is hard, through it all there is a hope in the future.

• **Fear**: As John Beckmann draws out, a vision of the future can be grotesque. Monsters linger around every camp-fire, but these monsters relate the quivering fears of real life.

Beyond these few stories there are millions more. All of us together, I believe can make the world a better place by pointing out our hopes and fears. I believe that by narrating our hopes and dreams of a better future to the community around us, we build that positive future itself. By speaking out, and giving ourselves a voice, we are acting as the creators of our own destiny.

If you want to share your voice and your story with us, please send it to us via twitter @cifiscape or directly to us at Cifiscape@onyxneon.com. These stories can point a way forward.

The stories in this anthology each point towards this process. In doing so, they highlight the process of change, and the chaos of democracy. It must be remembered we need people's shared visions, hope and fear to point our way in the darkness of what lays beyond our vision — be it monster or paradise. In other words, we need to walk like my father, teaching our children to dream; it leads to a lot of good things.

Kit Martin, Director of Cifiscape
Sunday, March 4th, 2012

## Learn More

Clinton, Bill. 2011. *Back to Work: Why We Need Smart Government for a Strong Economy.* Knopf.

Holstein, William J. 2011. *The Next American Economy: Blueprint for a Real Recovery.* Walker & Company.

Peter Diamandis: *Abundance is our future* | Video on TED.com. http://www.ted.com/talks/peter_dia mandis_abundance_is_our_future.html

Zinn, Howard. 2005. *A People's History of the United States: 1492 to Present.* Harper Perennial Modern Classics.

*Solve for X.* 2012. http://www.wesolveforx. com/#t=a&n=abab420b

# Acknowledgements

This book could not be made without a lot of people, too many to name all of here, but we would like to point out a few. To our father who we miss, our two  most wonderful ladies, Abbey and Mika, to make anything we need your support and care. The editors who poured over each story: Pat Edmonson, Hannah Byrns-Enoch, Crystal Boyd and most of all for Chastity West, each for being a champion and defender of the English language, which Kit, at least, tends to take his liberties with. In our darkest hour of over work, you pulled this book together again. Also for the Cifiscape community who gives us feedback every step of the way, and to our authors who work with us to improve their submissions and got back to us with rewrites, at times remarkably fast–I think the record was 20 minutes. We'd also like to thank you, for buying this book, and funding this local book project to go on. We love doing it, and we hope you love reading it.

*Jeffrey and Kit Martin*

# Harris

By Jonathan Hansen

Harris heard it before she did.

A clatter and crash. It echoed across the windswept rubble of Nicollet Avenue. Harris crouched in the shadow of a burnt-out tank and nocked an arrow. Boone did the same, no thought, just reflex. She shifted the big black duffel bag slung across her back. It hung heavy, stuffed to bulging and so, so important.

*Shit. Come on. Not now*, she thought. *We're almost home.*

But Harris waited, so she waited too.

The Ssysekian armada may have been gone, gone for months now, the skies over Minneapolis—over the whole world—empty of the great dark discs of their mother ships, but the hard-learned lessons remained.

Old memories in her head, Harris' gruff and gravel voice as

gleaming Ssysek attack ships swooped low and sowed the earth with thundering rows of fire. *You want to survive, you run.* The ground boomed. A haze of dust settled over them. Fighting didn't do shit. They won. We lost. We're nothing but rats in their house now. In her mind, she saw his crooked nose and his shock of white hair as he peered out from their hiding spot. Like her, he was as thin and ragged as an alley cat. *You hide and you wait and when the moment comes, you run.* He'd tell her this over and over again as the bombs fell and the whole world shook. *That's how you survive.*

So they waited.

Their breath fogged. The hazy, gray fall around them was very quickly sliding into the ashy-snowed winter to come. The wind howled through the broken skyscrapers. The towers creaked and swayed. Papers twirled down into the street like confetti.

The noise again. Closer. It was coming from across the street, from within the sagging ruin of Macy's. Inside, shafts of sunlight pierced the gloom like golden spears and Boone could see garbage and girders, crumbling stone and dripping water.

Something dashed through the light and shadows.

*Come on, be nothing, please. We're so goddamn close.* Her eyes drifted up, up, up the jagged silhouette of the IDS building. *I just want to get home…*

There was a rush of noise, stumbles and thuds.

A deer burst from one of the old display windows—a stag. Tattered rags hung from its antlers like clothes on the line. Its white chest heaved with hard breaths. It was slat-ribbed and dusty, its flank scarred. But it still stood tall and regal, still amazing, an old-world refugee. Its hooves click-clacked on the concrete.

Bambi, Boone gasped and right on top of that, Dinner, swamped by a flood of drooling hunger. She wanted to get home; she needed to get home, the weight of the bag across her back reminded her that she had to get home, but this? This was like winning the lottery. Fresh meat. She wanted to jump up and down and clap.

She squeaked giddily.

The stag spotted them across the intersection and froze.

"Steady," Harris said and stood, smooth and easy, careful not to spook the beast. She watched him raise his bow, his eyes slit in concentration. Hunger twisted in her guts, warring with a desperate need, with a vicious want. He would make the shot. He always made the shot. He had to make the shot.

But he grunted as he drew the bow. She saw it shake at the end of his arm. She tried to ignore it. *He's fine.* She thought. *He's fine.* Little things had been nagging at her lately, lots of little things, his hacking coughs in the morning, his groaning stretches and all of his aching, sore-ass complaints.

*He's not a young man anymore.*

She had wanted him to stay home today, but I've taken care of you too long to stop now, was his reply. Before the invasion, he had worked in a library. He loved that job. He couldn't wait to get to work. And once, when she was really little, he had shown her the heap of glass and steel that remained of it. She had tried not to cry as he knelt at the ruins because it always scared her when he did, but she had been too little and too confused, so she cried anyway. I lost them that day, my family, the day the Ssysek had come, wreathed in flames as they burned down through the atmosphere. I wasn't there. He had clutched at her. That's why we stick together now, understand? But all of that had been a long time ago and he hadn't been a young man then either.

"You ready, kid?" He whispered through clenched teeth.

She slipped out of the big duffel. It clinked on the concrete and slowly sagged over. She patted its side. *Don't go anywhere.*

The stag stood across Nicollet, behind an Army defensive line the Ssysek had long ago blasted to splinters and melted lumps of metal. It pranced. Its white tail flashed and its ears twitched.

"I'm ready," Boone whispered.

She eased her knife from its sheath. The tape wrapping the handle was frayed and sweat-darkened, but the blade gleamed in her dirty fist. She crouched, her old boots creaking. She wanted this. She needed this. She could almost smell the stag roasting on the spit, could almost hear the fat sizzle and pop. She was practically drooling for a taste.

She was ready.

Oh yeah, she was ready.

Fresh meat.

The stag would run. From fear and pain and shock, from the rush of adrenaline, the stag would run. Her job was to chase it and bring it down quick. Slit its throat. Harris would catch up—too old to keep up anymore—and they would do the rest together, fast: skin it, gut it, strip the meat, and hope that no dog packs lurked close by or any leopards stalked the skyscraper heights or worse…

A horn shattered the silence, a long echoing blast.

The stag scrambled into a run. It leapt the wreckage and bounded past them.

They exchanged a wide-eyed look.

"Hide!" Harris barked. They sprinted around the fire-blackened tank and ducked through the jagged hole blown in its armor. They crawled on hands and knees through sooty dark, dangling wires, and scorched and scattered bones.

Horns echoed in the concrete canyons.

She scooted back up against Harris. He wrapped a long, wiry arm around her. His scratchy cheek brushed her. "We're alright, it's okay," he whispered. "Shhh-shhh-shhh, we're just fine," but she could feel his heart hammering in his chest, his body thrumming with nervous energy.

There were shouts and crashes coming from Macy's. She couldn't see the store from this side of the tank, but she didn't have to. She knew what was coming. The noise tumbled out into the open air, suddenly louder, kicking through the rubble and trash that littered the street.

"They're hunting the stag," Boone whispered.

"I know," Harris shushed her.

The horn sounded again. It was long and loud and close.

A crowd broke over them, a howling pack; they leapt the tank in a sudden rush.

*The Broken.*

Once they had been survivors like her, like Harris and their friends, until the Ssysek Harvesters had scooped them up and into the endless rise and fall of the shuttles. Everything the Ssysek stole, their plundered loot—water, minerals, oil, and a pleading, screaming mass of humanity—it was all taken up into the waiting mother ships.

And it was all long gone now, gone with the Ssysek, carried off to the stars.

All except the Broken.

Occasionally, shuttles would land in the ruins. Their holds would spin open and people would stagger out, bent and mangled and blinking in the mealy gray light of day. The return of the Broken. Ssysekian Marauders would follow them out, clanking in their heavy gray armor and fishbowl helmets sloshing with a yellow liquid. They would jab with long sparking prods, screeching their weird cicada-chirps and the Broken would scatter before them, loosed upon the world.

And now they hunted the ruins, chasing whatever would run.

The stag had gotten turned around inside the remains of an old Barnes & Noble. Boone could see it from her hiding spot. She could hear it crashing about. It was trapped behind the broken counter of the coffee bar. It bleated and turned, nostrils flared and eyes wide. Its antlers tangled in the sagging chandelier.

The Broken thudded up and over the wreckage, barking and stinking and stomping. They dragged their rebar spears, metal sparking in the street. They slipped in through the wall of empty windows, creeping among the toppled shelves and rotting piles of rain-pulped books.

They rushed in.

They bellowed and hooted, ecstatic. They stabbed over the counter. The big stag kicked and screamed. They tackled it, their weight dragging the beast down. They reared up and hit it with hunks of concrete, again and again, blood splattering.

Boone counted twelve. "We should go," she whispered. They had lost the stag—there was no need to stay.

"Quiet," Harris shushed her again. "Wait."

Boone was quick with her blade. Growing up she'd had to be. Ssysekian Marauders had been tough and in the narrow confines of the ruins they were murder machines, but underneath their armor, they were the softest of flesh. A quick jab and the skin would part with a plop, like a lanced boil, spewing a piss-warm spray and a choking sulfur stink. Then they would screech and thrash. Their eye-stalks would wilt and their oily skin would dry and crack and seep a thick black gunk as their bodies contorted and their cries trailed off into agonized, spitting clicks. It was easy, if you were quick.

Boone had killed her share over the years.

And when she did, she left their corpses to be found by their kind. She had survived the reprisals too, hunkered down in the ruins, hiding from the monstrous Tick-tock hunters and the orbital bombardments that shook the city. She had outlasted it all. She had stood in the rubble the day the mother ships flew away. She had felt the deep bass thrum of their engines press against her, spiraling up whirls of dust.

She was a survivor.

So she wasn't afraid of a few Broken. She had faced them before, dangerous, yeah, especially in large packs, but in the end, nothing but animals. She could take four, if she was fast. Maybe more, if she was lucky and the ground favored her. Yeah, she flexed her fingers, Four, easy. But twelve? Out in the open?

No, it was time to run, before their luck ran out, before the Broken found them.

The pack huddled around the stag, the big ones closed in, the small ones jostling around the edges. The stag quivered and jerked and bled. The Broken slurped and grunted and muttered and munched, dressed in faded skins, purple rags and tattered hoodies. They were a twisted and hobbled bunch, every one of them maimed and cut and grafted with tangles of strange alien metal.

The biggest one was bald and wore a broken horned helmet. His back was to Boone. It was a mess of scars and metal and matted with coarse curls of gray hair from his shoulders to his dirty ass crack. He squatted in the middle of the group and ate slow and assured. The others gave him plenty of space.

Twelve was too many. "Let's go," Boone whispered.

Harris shushed her.

She had to get home. Her head was pounding. She swallowed, her throat etched with nervous acid. *They can't find us. We have to get home.* She still heard Tonya in her nightmares, the terrified screaming as a pack of Broken dragged her from her hiding spot. She had screamed and screamed and she didn't stop until they had smashed her head in with a hunk of concrete. Boone clenched her shaking hands into fists, adrenaline burning through her. *I have to get home. I have to. I can't get caught out here. I have...*

"The bag," she gasped. "Oh, shit, Harris! The bag. I left it..."

He shushed her again, a harsh hissing slice of noise, a little too loud.

A blood-streaked head popped up out of the huddle.

They both froze.

The man was butt-chinned and wide-nosed beneath a rat's nest of black hair salted with gray. An old tie draped his bare chest and bloodstained shirtsleeves bunched up at his wrists. He stared around slow and suspicious. Then he nudged Horn-head, who turned on his haunches and looked around, squinty-eyed, and slowly chewing, his chin blood-streaked and dribbling. He finally shrugged and the duo sank back into the huddle.

Boone exhaled relief.

"They know we're here," Harris said.

"What? No, I don't—"

"Watch."

She did. She watched them snuffle and gnaw on sloppy, bloody fistfuls. She watched close and realized their eating had slowed. Then she saw their eyes, the sidelong glances and the slow and careful hands dragging their rebar spears up off the concrete.

"Shit."

"Get the bag," Harris said, "and keep going. The Bancorp building is right behind us across the street. Go inside and up the escalators. Cut across the skyway to Macy's and then over Nicollet into the IDS and…"

"No," she said.

"…get home."

"No!"

"I'll slow 'em down."

"No!"

He put a hand on her shoulder, "Boone, I'll catch up."

She gasped.

A sudden crash of memory. What will we call it? Danny's voice in her head. She remembered how he had touched tiny toes and tiny fingers, his easy smile and blue-blue eyes, his hands so rough and his touch so soft. He brushed errant strands of dishwater hair from her eyes. I'll catch up, he had said. She remembered the chaos and confusion of that day, south of the Cities, the tide of refugees. She remembered crouching behind meager shelter, the smoking wreckage that had once been a Cabella's. She remembered riotous thunder, the last ditch effort of the Army's cannons, the distant blooms of fire. Most of all, she remembered the line of Ssysek Harvesters, still coming, big treads tearing up the countryside, a storm of churned earth and snatching tentacles. Don't worry. It was the last thing he ever said to her. I'll catch up.

"We stick together," she spat, shaking Harris off.

Bam, bam, bam.

They stopped.

Bam, bam, bam. Horn-head was rapping the tile with his rebar. It was tipped with a big hunk of concrete. Bam, bam, bam. The others joined in, spears ringing on metal and water-warped wood. Tang, tang, tang. Bang, bang, bang. They turned toward the broken tank with bloody, jagged-tooth grins. Bam, bam, bam.

Harris gave her a hard look. "Don't wait for me."

He shoved past her, out into the street.

The Broken surged up, their spears rattling. One woman rushed forward, ruddy and blonde and pig-faced. She was wearing a filthy, oversized purple shirt with a big number seven across the front. It hung on her like a blood-drenched dress.

She threw her spear.

Harris leaned to one side.

The spear clanged off the tank and bounced away.

He straightened, nocked an arrow from the quiver on his hip. He drew his bow and released. Jersey-dress yelped. She stumbled and fell, a shaft sticking out of her thigh. He nocked another and fired. He drew a third, aimed and released.

The Broken scattered.

"Run, Boone!"

She burst out of the tank and around its scorched sides. The bow sang behind her. She heard a howl of pain. She scooped up the duffel bag and threw it over her shoulder as she ran. She leapt over the broken planters and their spill of dry soil and dead trees, threading the decorative stone garden that littered the front of the building. A spear squealed past, scraping a white chalk line across one big rock, and she dove through the lobby door. She tumbled over a carpet of dead leaves. The lobby was open, the ceiling soared above her and a balcony looked down. The escalators were mangled and leaning.

She staggered to her feet and started climbing.

Harris stumbled in. He nocked an arrow and let it fly. Spears banged off the cracked tiles around him. From the balcony, Boone could see six Broken lurking in the wreckage out on the street, keeping low. Harris kept shooting, arrows clattering off metal. She could see only two or three more shafts rolling around the edges of his quiver.

"Come on!" She shouted.

He looked up at her. "I'm coming, go!" He was flushed and sweating, breathing heavily. His arm shook as he drew and released. She heard a yelp.

"Harris," she said. "Please. Come."

"Boone, damn it! I will catch up!" He barked, nocked an arrow, and drew.

Rebar punched through him, a twisted stick of rusty iron. He grunted, the arrow skipping off the lobby floor. Blood dribbled the spear's length and spattered the tile. He dropped to his knees and fell over onto his side. A slow crimson pool spread beneath him.

Boone couldn't move. She couldn't even scream.

She pressed dirty hands to her face.

Horn-head roared in, slamming his hammer down. Harris' body flopped. He struck again and Boone heard bone snapping. Jersey-dress limped in, the arrow still in her leg. She yanked the spear out of Harris and held it aloft, screeching bloody victory at the ceiling. The others joined in. A red-polo wearing brute, naked from the waist down, saw Boone at the balcony's edge above him and threw his spear.

She ducked and it bounced and clanged somewhere behind her.

She ran. She didn't look back.

Spears slammed into the rotted wall panels, thunk, thunk, thunk. They stuck, quivering. *You have to get home. You have to. That's all that matters now.* She didn't think about Harris. She couldn't. Home. She focused on home. The heavy duffel clinked. It pulled at her, the hard edges poking. The skyway was just ahead.

Clang!

A spear bounced off the floor next to her and skittered away. She stumbled.

Whack!

Another smacked into a pillar as she raced past, spraying her with stone chips. She ducked aside.

Thud!

She was punched in the back and knocked off her feet. She hit the floor in a sliding tangle. The duffel bag smacked her in the back of the head, her face smacked the tile. Something cold and wet soaked her, it slicked the tile. She pushed herself up on her hands and twisted around, wincing at the throb in her ribs. She looked over her shoulder.

A rebar spear was sticking straight up out of the bag.

It had pierced one side, but not the other. The bag had slowed it down. Her ribs ached where it had thudded into her, tight and stinging, but...

*At least I'm not dead.*

She slipped off the bag and yanked the spear free. It came loose with a squealing scrape of metal on metal and a spurt of sticky-sweet liquid. Clumps of yellow cake clung to the rusty shaft. She tossed it aside and reshouldered the bag.

Running feet.

*Shit! Get up! Get up!*

She lurched up, but the man in the red polo was right on her. He lunged in. She caught his wrist and pulled herself up, yanking on him hard, turning and letting go. The man went by in a running fall. His feet slipped on the wet tile and he tumbled—bare ass and red polo—out the open window without a sound.

Tie guy was right behind him.

He grabbed at her and she ducked, shoving at him. He caught the bag. *No!* He spun her around and threw her, tearing the bag away.

"No! Damn it!"

She hit the floor, hands out and rolling. Her boots caught. She came up with her knife and rushed back in. The blade bit deep. Tie guy grunted. She felt the edge scrape bone and she ripped it free. Hot blood splashed down her arm, across her face. She snatched the big bag back from him as he stutter-stepped away. He stared at his blood-soaked palms, stared at her, and then a ropey red tangle hit the tile with a splat.

He fell.

And she was running again, slinging the duffel back over her shoulders.

She sprinted across the sagging open frame of the skyway. It creaked and groaned. It wobbled under her boots. There were holes in the floor and the street below was piled with rubble. Fluttering rags of old carpet whipped about like tattered flags.

Heavy footsteps were coming up fast behind her, shaking the bridge.

She dropped.

Horn-head stumbled over her, swinging wildly. His hammer struck the metal frame, the hunk of concrete shattering. The skyway shook. Boone scrambled back on her butt, awkward and shuffling, the duffel bag slowing her down again, getting in her way. She heard metal screech and snap beneath her. Ping! Again. Ping! The bridge shuddered beneath her, the shakes getting harder. Horn-head roared, swinging his length of rebar. She rolled the side as he slammed it down. The skyway groaned, long and loud, and the frame started to twist and tip.

Horn-head fell back, scrambling for something to grab onto. Boone rolled over and raced for the skyway's end and the dark, waiting hole of Macy's. A shrieking din of tearing metal built all around her.

The skyway dropped out from beneath her, sudden open air beneath her toes.

She leapt.

And hit dirty tile, she scrabbled at the edges, pulling herself in. Brick and metal crashed down behind her. It boomed in the street. A cloud of dust and debris blasted up in a gritty, choking fist. She rolled up onto solid ground.

She laid there a moment, catching her breath, and then raised her head to a world of quiet, chalky white. She was sprawled out just inside Macy's, inches from the broken edge. She stood, slow and coughing, with her toes at the drop. She hefted the duffel bag and looked down into the ruined street.

The wind swept the dust away in great swirling swaths. The wreckage of the skyway emerged from the murk like a ship from the fog. It was laying across the street, spread between the two buildings, a jumble of rubble and rusted metal. There was blood splashed everywhere. Then she saw him.

Horn-head stood in the street and glowered up at her.

"Son of a…" She breathed ragged disbelief.

Her hands were empty. She'd lost her knife. "Shit."

His helmet was gone and he was dusted completely white from head to toe, save for the bright red cuts and trickles. His right arm was broken, jagged bone poking through torn skin. He clutched bent rebar in his left hand. He stared at Boone with black hatred.

Tick-tick-tick-tick-tick…rum-rumble-rumble…

The street—the rubble, the concrete and twisted metal—it

heaved up and lurched.

Tick-tick-tick-tick-tick-tick-tick…

Boone gasped. *No! That's not possible!* She saw Horn-head spin, staring at the ground, animal terror contorting his scarred face. *They're all gone!* Cold panic drenched her and she stepped back from the edge.

The rubble moved again, rising and falling, scraping and sliding.

Tick-tick-tick-tick-tick-tick-tick-tick-tick…

*There's no Tick-tock Hunters left!*

A spiked metal ball punched up through the concrete. It was big and dented and attached to a snaking metal arm. More arms burst loose. Pincers grabbed. Saws screeched and bit into the rubble. They smashed at it. They tore at it. They threw it aside. A tentacle ratcheted out and wrapped around Horn-head. The links tick-tick-tick tightened down. He screamed and squirmed, his arms pinned to his sides.

Boone ran.

Tick-tick-tick-tick-tick-tick…

His screams grew louder. They chased her into the gloom of Macy's, past rubble and ruin and forgotten things, through shafts of weak sunlight. She ran for the bright light shining across the room—the Nicollet skyway. *Come on, come on, come on.*

Tick-tick-tick-tick-tick-tick…

She heard a wet bursting pop and then no more screams.

An explosion boomed in the street behind her, metal clanking and dragging against stone. Boone hit the floor and slid around the corner. She pressed her back up against the wall. She swallowed, flushed and gasping, her heart trying to hammer its way out of her chest. She steadied the duffel bag and peeked back the way she had come. She watched the ragged hole, hoping no tentacles appeared, probing, hunting.

She waited.

*Nothing. Hmmm...*

She could hear it clanking. She crawled out onto the skyway and peeked.

Tick-tick-tick-tick-tick—sqwark!—tick-tick-hhhhhhh-hhsssssssss-tick...

The Tick-tock Hunter lumbered out into the intersection, a nightmare machine of waving tentacles and click-clack metal spider legs, the Ssysekian scourer of worlds.

But it had seen better days.

It was a rusted ruin, grinding metal and dragging broken legs. Half of its eyestalks were broken. Its guns were bent and fire-blackened.

*It's junk*, she realized, *it's nothing but left behind junk.*

Tick-tick...tick...t...ti... ti...t-t-t-t...

The Hunter collapsed in a heap, clanging and winding down. It shuddered and shook and slowed. Wispy tendrils of smoke crept from its broken carapace and the wind pulled the hazy gray ribbons to tatters.

And then the world was quiet again.

"Thank fucking God," she gasped.

*Run.*

She was up and sprinting across the creaking skyway and into the sun-streaked cavern at the foot of the IDS tower. A massive metal framework domed overhead, rusty and dusty and filled with the hushed quiet of the coming dusk. The decorative trees had long ago gone wild. Branches twined among the rafters. They wrapped the walkways and smashed into the old shops. The floor was carpeted with dead leaves and twinkling shards of glass.

The IDS tower loomed overhead, shadowed and broken.

They'd been camping in the tower's upper reaches all summer. Most of the stairs were still intact and only some were exposed to the elements. She had to scale the last few floors, clinging to crumbling platforms, her toes wedged in the cracks and her body straining as she hauled herself up. Pebbles clicked and clacked and clattered all the long way back down the dark stairwell. She only paused at the top, fifty-one flights, and then she sat there, her legs dangling out over the well as she caught her breath.

The tower swayed, the wind keening through the open floors.

The stairwell door was crammed with broken desks and piled chairs. She got down on her knees and crawled beneath, pushing the heavy duffel before her and out into the open floor beyond.

She was finally home.

"Welcome back," Scott waited on the far side. She could see his round face and the frayed collar of his dirty fatigues as he crouched behind an overturned desk. He still shaved his head high and tight, still a soldier. He pointed his battered M4 at the ceiling. It was probably loaded with all four bullets he had left. "I was starting to get worried."

"Hey," Boone stood, dusting herself off. "She awake?"

"Is that thing full?" Scott gasped, swinging himself out and around the desk.

His legs ended at the knees.

"Yeah," she kicked the bag. "Lots of cans. A few Twinkies. Is she awake?"

He scooted over, hands and stumps, hands and stumps, the rifle slung across his back. He was focused on the big duffel. "She's in the bassinet. How much did we get?"

"Plenty…" Boone dunked her hands into one of their rain barrels, the water icy cold. She scrubbed, sluicing off the blood, and left Scott digging in the bag, errant silver cans rolling across the floor.

The middle office was protected by four walls and the bassinet was a filing cabinet drawer stuffed with blankets and coats—anything soft and warm they could find.

The baby was snuggled down within and wrapped in an old sweater. She gurgled and cooed up at Boone, her arms happily reaching. She had dishwater blonde hair like her mama and blue-blue eyes like her father. Their sweet summer child. Boone knelt down next to her, sniffing and smiling and blinking back happy tears.

"Hey baby," she whispered, "Mama's home."

"Hey, where's…" Scott started to call out but then trailed off.

She lifted the baby. It kicked and babbled and Boone held her close, pressing her face into the child's soft, sweet-smelling warmth. little fingers curled in her hair, pulling. She sat cross-legged by the office door, cradling the baby, and looked out over the broken topple of the Twin Cities.

A chill wind cut in.

The hazy smear of the sun touched the horizon and the clouds lit up, slashing the sky with pinks and oranges and deep reds. A blanket of shadow settled over the ruins, the sludgy trickle of the Mississippi a dark ribbon, gray skies sliding into black.

Scott dragged himself over, an awkward one-handed slide, and held out a fork and a scuffed and dented silver can, the lid bent back. There were sliced peaches in sauce within. "The Twinkies were pulped, man," he reported.

"Those Twinkies saved my life, man," she said.

"And it's cold as shit up here today," he said, scooting around, sitting next to her.

"Yep," she said. "We're gonna have to ditch this place soon, find someplace new, someplace warmer… safer, maybe leave the city."

He grunted and motioned first at his legs, then at the baby, and then up at Boone. A raised eyebrow, "How're we gonna do that?"

She looked at him, squinting in the last glare of the setting sun. "We'll stick together," she said and winked. Then she mashed a bit of peach between her fingers and slipped it into the baby's smiling mouth. "I thought of a name."

"Yeah?" He had a silver can of his own. It looked like corn.

"Finally," he teased.

"It had to be right," Boone said. She was still smiling. She couldn't seem to help herself anymore, not when she was home. "A new baby. A new world. It had to be right."

"So?" He said around a mouthful of corn. "Let's hear it."

"Harris," she said. "I'm going to name her Harris."

"For a girl?" Scott raised an eyebrow.

"Shut up," she smirked and mashed a bit of peach at him. "It's a good name. She should know him...him and her father. Harris Daniel Ruin-runner."

He chewed and thought and finally shrugged. "Alright. Good name."

"Good name," Boone agreed and slipped peach mush into little Harris' mouth.

# The Rotations of The Earth

## By David Oppegaard

After the Russians launched the intrepid Yuri Gagarin and Vostok 1 into space in 1961, Danny Haskell's mother sat up on their couch late into the night, watching the news on TV, then listening to BBC radio when all the TV stations went off the air. She absorbed every fresh report in attentive silence, her restless hands knitting a scarf that would end up a good six feet long. Danny, only seven years old at the time, sat up with his mother as long as he could before sleepiness overcame him, trying to understand why a lady in Akron, Ohio, cared so much about some Rusky she'd never even met.

Eventually, Danny would come to understand that Yuri had been the first human being in space, ever, and what an event like that would mean to someone like his mother, who loved anything that had to do with space, space ships, and futuristic cities loaded with gleaming skyscrapers and zipping tubes of public transport. Lynn Haskell read bright-eyed sci-fi authors like Ray Bradbury and Isaac Asimov and she thought that, at the latest, the American automotive industry would invent a reasonably priced flying car by 1979. At dinnertime, over mashed potatoes and pork chops, or her famous hamburger goulash, she often brought up subjects like "terraforming" other planets, five-dimensional space, wormhole pathways, atomic mutation, and the space-time continuum.

Danny's mother also believed modern science would allow her to live long enough to see her grandchildren, her great-grandchildren, and her great-great-grandchildren. She bought sturdy Ethan Allen furniture, expensive Sterling flatware, and clothing with tough, construction worker-like qualities—rivet buttoned pants made out of thick canvas, peasant shirts with triple stitching, and no-frills, magazine-ordered underwear the manufacturer claimed would last you a lifetime. She took her vitamins, drank carrot juice, and walked four miles four times a week, often making Danny and his two older sisters accompany her, the three Haskell children bored out of their skulls as they passed the same old neighborhood trees, houses, and yapping dogs while their mother watched the sky, her eyes clear and searching.

Lynn Haskell liked to say the future waited for no man, which Danny thought was one of those sayings that made sense as long as you didn't think about it too much.

Danny's father, Bo Haskell, was a heavy drinker who worked as tax auditor for the IRS. Bo had broad shoulders, a rock hard paunch, and kept his hair cut in a rigid flattop you could have bounced a quarter off (if you were feeling fast and lucky). Whenever he was feeling surly, which was often, Bo liked to ask his wife what the hell she thought she was doing, wasting her time with all this airy-fairy, futuristic crap. Sometimes young Danny would be in the room for these discussions, sitting at the kitchen table as he played with his toy robots or, later, read Sports Illustrated. Danny could never tell if his father was serious when he began these inquiries or if he was just bored with whatever was on TV and looking to argue.

"It's pretty simple, Bo," Danny's mother would respond, touching her wavy, chestnut colored hair, which she liked to wear down and considered her best feature. "I'm planning for the future."

"But what about our now? Can't we just enjoy our now, with our regular gasoline cars that don't fly and our regular lives that last about seventy, eighty years?"

"Sure we can. And I do."

"But it's not enough for you? You need more than right now, huh?"

Danny's mother would cross her arms at this point, if she hadn't done so already.

"I just want us to be prepared, Bo. As a family, I want us to embrace change and meet every challenge head-on. I've told you before—we should all be prepared to live a long time. Modern medicine has made some amazing advances already. Just imagine what it'll do in twenty or thirty years."

Here, Danny's father would nod and pretend to imagine.

"Okay, I'll give you science and medicine, but I just don't think they're going to make us immortal."

"Not immortal, Bo. Long lived. Like in the Old Testament."

"So you think we'll live to be nine hundred years old?"

"No, nine hundred is a bit of a stretch. But I wouldn't be surprised if we both hit one-fifty."

"Jesus," his father would say, throwing his hands into the air. "I don't think I could handle that, Lynnie. Would we have to be married that long? Or do you think we could work some sort of trade-in, swap-out thing around eighty? Like buying a new car or something?"

"Very funny, sweetie, but I don't think your great-grand-children would approve of that kind of sentiment. I think they'd be pretty offended by it, actually."

"Right. And how am I supposed to remember everybody's damn name in this future of yours?"

A smile, not particularly friendly, would creep across his mother's face.

"I'll create a chart with pictures, dear. We can put it up on the fridge, so every time you go for a beer, you'll see it. That should keep your memory pretty fresh, don't you think? You'll probably memorize all their birthdays, too."

From here, the conversation usually passed on to his father's drinking, then to his father's boring job, then to neither of them giving a damn about anything, anyway. Danny would either zone out or depart from the room long before these conversations fizzled to their inevitable conclusion, his parents retreating to their respective corners of the house to seethe and plot their next move, leaving in their wake a deep, muffled silence not unlike the vacuum of outer space.

By 1967, Danny's older sisters had grown breasts and refused to go on any more neighborhood walks with their mother, citing the unbearable embarrassment at being seen in public with their square family. Danny's mother took this change in stride, as if further evidence of the future rolling upon them all, and seemed satisfied with the company of her youngest alone as they continued their walks. Danny, now thirteen, felt an inkling of familial embarrassment himself, but he pushed these feelings away, unwilling to imagine a world in which his mother had to walk alone through the city. Too many bad things could happen: his mother might get hit by a car, mugged by a hooligan, or just keep walking and walking, until she left Canton behind for good, like a helium balloon cut loose.

They didn't talk much on their walks. Danny learned to walk and watch at the same time, his conscious thoughts receding while his mind absorbed the world around him. The city didn't seem as dull anymore, now that his sisters weren't around to point out how boring it was every two minutes. If you listened closely, you could hear the wind shaking the trees, the creaking of unlatched fences. You noticed all the rabbits hiding in the tall grass, noses twitching, and the cats slowly stalking them from a distance. You could even feel the earth moving beneath your feet, rotating just slowly enough that it didn't fling you into space like a dog shaking itself dry.

Once, when they'd stopped at a drug store to buy Creamsicles, his mother asked Danny what he thought his life would be like in fifty years.

"What do you mean?"

"I mean, how do you envision the distant years ahead, Mr. Danny Haskell? What will the future hold for you, personally?"

"I don't know. I'll get a job, probably. Buy a house."

"Beyond that, I mean. Beyond all that boring, run-of-the-mill stuff. Do you think you'll be able to teleport around the planet? Or take weekend trips to Mars to visit your grandkids?"

"I guess so," Danny said, nibbling at the melting edges of his orange Creamsicle. "But I don't know much about science, really."

"And you think I do? I'm a housewife who never went to college—NASA isn't exactly pounding on my door to beg for my help. Not unless they need someone to change a diaper, or bake a pan of lasagna."

His mother laughed and Danny took a big bite out of his Creamsicle, which was starting to melt. They'd left the drug store and headed in the general direction of home. His mother hadn't started eating her ice cream yet—she kept waving it around in the air like a traffic cop.

"I like your lasagna, Mom. It's the best."

"Thanks, honey, but that's not my point. I'm saying you've got to keep your eyes open so you can see the possibilities ahead of you. You don't need to live in Ohio your whole life tied down to the same house and job. You're still young, Danny. So much stuff is going to happen in your lifetime, you won't believe it."

Danny finished his Creamsicle, nibbling the stubborn ice cream remnants from the flat wooden stick. He wondered about what parts of the future he wouldn't believe and why. It seemed to him that his mother was right, that anything was possible, but that whatever did happen would, in the end, seem inevitable. He'd graduate from high school, maybe go to college, get a job, and get hitched. In that way, the future wouldn't be so different from the past. Billions of people had lived before him, billions of people would live after him. If you forgot about the space ships and the flying cars, the future sounded a lot like the present.

By the following spring, Lynn Haskell had stopped talking much about stuff like Star Trek and *1984* and how the future was marching upon them. Danny's mother claimed to have entered more of a *Brave New World* phase, which apparently meant taking a lot of prescription pills and baking way too many cookies. The pills made her eyes foggy and distant and the cookies made her gain weight, her normally trim figure thickening until Danny's father started making little piggy jokes.

Then, in an effort to get out of the house more, his mother started taking an art class at the community college. She came home from the second session crying, mascara running down her cheeks as she chucked her art supplies into the trash. When his father shouted that those things had cost good money, goddamn it, his mother fled the kitchen and locked herself in the bathroom at the back of the house. Danny's sisters took turns talking to their mother through the bathroom door, cooing to her as if she were a wounded badger capable of lashing out at any moment. Finally, after two long hours, they got her to unlock the door and go lie down, everybody in the house exhausted by the whole ordeal.

After quitting her community art class, his mother stopped going on walks around their neighborhood, no matter how much Danny prodded her to go with him. A creature of habit, Danny began going on walks by himself, enmeshed in thought as the budding Akron trees slowly greened and the occasional car zoomed by. Sometimes he would turn to his right, wanting to say something, to make some funny observation, only to catch himself just before speaking, his mouth already open.

One afternoon in early May, Danny came home from school to find his house empty and silent. By some rare twist of scheduling, both of his older sisters were out, his father hadn't come home from work yet, and his mother was nowhere to be seen. Glad to have the house to himself for once, Danny shrugged off his backpack and headed for the bathroom, hoping to get in at least five solid minutes of masturbation before someone came home and started poking around.

As he made his way to the back of the house, Danny noticed the door to his parents' bedroom was cracked open. This was strange because usually their door was either totally open or totally closed. Danny knocked on the door and nudged it further open with his foot (if he was going to manhandle himself, he didn't want any surprises. It was bad enough that his mother had found his labor intensive collage of Playboy photographs the year before and replaced his naked ladies with a picture of himself as an innocent, smiling baby).

"Hello? Anybody here?"

The bedroom drapes were drawn, the room dark and murky. An elongated lump, the shape of his mother sleeping beneath a floral patterned comforter, rose up on the left side of the bed.

"Oh. Sorry, Mom."

Danny was about to duck out and close the door behind him when something on his mother's dresser caught his eye. It was a bottle of bourbon whiskey, his father's preferred beverage of choice after five PM. The whiskey, uncapped and half-empty, was sitting beside an empty bottle of sleeping pills. Also on the dresser was one of Danny's old toys, a yellow plastic rocket ship he'd played with as a little boy, making the takeoff and landing sounds himself, filling their living room with the sound of swooshes, explosions, and engine fire.

Danny had not seen or thought about the rocket ship in years.

He turned around, suddenly wishing he'd never come into the bedroom at all. He sat on the edge of his parents' bed, the rocket ship clenched in his hand, and watched how his mother's chest did not rise and fall beneath the comforter as she did not breathe. He would think about this moment, and his mother, for the rest of his life, deep into the unimaginable future, where the fog of speculation would be replaced by certainty, by years lived and homes bought and sold, by three children and two beautiful ex-wives, by gleaming cities and plasma TVs and sleek cars that did not fly (though they would talk to you and offer directions). And, when he himself lay on the edge of death in the far and distant year of 2012, his fifty-eight-year-old body overrun by a cancer even modern medicine could not defeat, Danny Haskell would ponder Yuri Gagarin, that daredevil Russian cosmonaut, and wonder if he'd felt a slight tugging, a moment of terrible, heart-rending loneliness, as he, too, was propelled from the earth.

# Lethal Options
## By Aaron M. Wilson

*What if we are a gear in a great machine, a perfect ma-
chine, a machine without soul humming and
whirring perfectly since clicked on. That would be something grand indeed. Grand! Yes, grand! Yet, it's more likely
that we're the rust corroding that great machine, brining it,
finally, to a sudden and jarring halt.*

- Christopher "Pugsley" Henderson,
The Greenway Prophet

Between deaths, I was given a choice. To my recollection, I was no one special. I was just a guy who liked to fix-up and sell old bicycles. In life, I had been known as Daniel Seward. I was something of a local hero, a second father to many troubled teenagers. When everyone in Minneapolis had given up on some delinquent, I would step forward and say, "Let me give it a go. I've yet to come across a bad apple I couldn't squeeze some sweetness from." It was true. I'd take anyone in the system and transform him or her into a pillar of the community. Perhaps, I was given the choice because I could see the good amidst the bad, but whomever, whatever, chose me to help set humanity's course was wrong about me.

When I woke from that first death, my mind was foggy as if I'd indulged too much. I felt high, ethereal, and not fully cooked. The details—the how's, why's, what's, and when's—were unclear. What I do remember from those first moments will haunt me for eternity, and if I had them to do again, I would have made a different choice. I should have made different choices.

Standing beside me was an old friend. He looked at me from under thick white eyebrows. His mustache flowed over both his lips, and he wore tight bike hat with the brim flipped up. I couldn't believe it, but there he was. It was Christopher "Pugsley" Henderson, The Greenway Prophet, the man who'd sold me the shop years ago and told me to take his name down and put mine up—that I'd never regret buying the shop. And I never did. Never.

"It's Boo's," said Pugsley. He waited.

"What is?"

"The shop."

"Who's Boo?" I asked. "And what kind of name is that anyway?"

Pugsley jerked his thumb over his shoulder. "Him."

I looked around him and saw a large man with long purple hair working on a road bike. I could tell my shop was in good hands by the loving way he pulled the tire from the rim, making sure not to damage the inner tube.

"You ready?" Pugsley asked as he took my hand.

I turned around. "For what?"

"Move on." He bobbed his head in the direction of the front door. The door disappeared and became a portal of light. "Yeah. Now, that's sweet. So, so, sweet."

I half expected him to lay down one of his famous "mans" on me, but he didn't.

"No." I said.

He looked at me with wide eyes and shook his head. The door that was solid light was a plain old door again. The street was visible through it.

Pugsley let go of my hand. "Rust. If you stay too long, you'll rust, man." There it was. He could stretch out the word "man" like no other, so it sounded more like a cow mooing than a person speaking.

"I need to see."

Pugsley shook his head like a mangy dog. Then the shop

began to melt away. First, Pugsley popped out of existence. He was there, and then he wasn't. Next, the bikes closest to me faded into in a cloud of steam. The cloud of steam expanded outward, until all I could see was a dense cloud.

"Hey hey," said a tall black man with a shaved head wearing a yellow bike shirt that clung to his leanly muscled frame. "Time to go for a ride," He produced two road bikes from thin air.

I didn't know if he'd just asked me a question that he wanted an answer to or if he was still having fun at my expense. Either way, he had my full attention. "Wait! Are you Yohann Gene, the first black man to ride in the Tour de France?"

"No, silly, I'm dead. Same as you." He looked at the bikes he was holding and the tight yellow jersey. "I see how you can make that mistake."

"Sorry. I don't mean any…"

"None taken. To be a first, now that would have been grand. This is not about me. It's about you." He pushed one of the road bikes to me, and I took it before it fell. "Time to ride."

"Wait!" I pointed to my shop. "What about it?"

"You're a silly man." He shook his head. "It's not good to be here much longer. Rust, man. Rust." He mounted his bike and rode off motioning me to follow.

As we pedaled, things got blurry, and before I knew it, I was riding down a bike lane along with thirty or forty others. We were all naked. I don't remember when I'd lost my clothes, but I was completely nude. Both the men and women who rode around me were in the buff singing songs with lyrics that I didn't recognize, but the music reminded me of REM's song about happy people, holding hands, and smiling. The atmosphere was infectious.

I sped up to the man who'd given me the bike. He was talking with a large-breasted woman with impossibly large areoles and nipples. She was riding a single-speed Surly, chestnut brown with white handle grips with matching tires and cables for a rear-wheel hand brake. Her bike looked like it was kept in good condition and cared for as if it were her lover.

"So…what's going on," I asked. I made sure my eyes focused on his face and then her face.

She turned to me with a funny look. "Nude ride. What does it look like?" She rode ahead of us.

"Thanks!" I called after her.

"Look," said the black man, "You just need to ride for a while. See what you see and then you'll move on." He shifted gears and was gone. He powered ahead to catch up with the woman on the single-speed Surly. She smiled as he pulled up beside her.

I tried to stop focusing on the people and bikes around me, but it was hard to ignore them. Drawn to each shiny bike as if my eyes were moths and the bikes beacons of hope, I barely noticed the people riding them.

I started by taking in the route we were riding. We were in the street. It was sometime at night, long after the sun had gone down and the streetlights had illuminated. The lanes on this street narrowed as if they'd been designed for bikes and not for cars. Instead of one or two lanes in one direction, there were four separated by dashed white lines, while a solid double yellow provided a median for directional traffic. As we passed through an intersection, I noticed that the cross streets were also divided four-by-four and packed with naked people on bikes intent on joining our group.

We turned left. A huge parking lot was off to our right, except that instead of car-sized parking stalls, there were rows and rows of metal bike stands. Each stand had at least two or three bikes locked up. When we reached the next corner, I realized that we'd just ridden by the grocery store where Lagoon splits off of Lake Street and becomes a one way: Lake Street east bound and Lagoon west bound. We were taking Lagoon west toward Hennepin, and I was waiting for the cops to pull us over. We were naked in public, after all.

We passed movie theaters and the Walker Library as everyone started to coast down the hill to Lake Calhoun. Each time we passed a parking lot or a side street, I saw more of the same. All of the streets that were once used for automotive traffic had been converted into bike lanes and all of the parking lots into bike corrals. I didn't know what utopia I'd died and woken up in, but if everyone could ride around naked and cars were a thing of the past, I could stay put here forever. I approved.

However, as we rounded Lake Calhoun, taking Excelsior toward St. Louis Park, the utopia turned into an automotive nightmare. Cars as far I could see sat gridlocked on a large overpass that skirted around Minneapolis. Seeing all of those cars created a rock hard spot in my stomach.

I turned to an older man and asked, "What's all that?"

"The Minneapolis bypass, it takes motorists around the city, but not into it." He went back to riding, but I had more questions.

"So, I have to admit, I'm new. What's going on?"

"We're a critical mass. We're protesting the new mayor's decision to allow cars back into the city. We had fifteen years of car-free traffic, thanks to Daniel Seward. Minneapolis is the world's most bike friendly and innovative city. I thought critical masses were dead here. No need really. But now, it seems we need to ride again."

I had to ask. "Daniel Seward?"

"Killed years ago in a car accident. He owned a bike shop. The city rallied around his death."

I nodded, and he rode ahead. "So… in a car accident."

We rode for a few miles more, around the far side of Lake Calhoun and down Excelsior, before coming to a clogged intersection near a popular grocery store chain known for its cheaply packed foods and wines based in California, not far from Highway 100.

We were forced onto the sidewalk by motor traffic and the abrupt end of the bike only streets. Riding on the sidewalk meant riding single file, a mile long parade of flesh on two wheels. When we came to a stop, I was shocked.

I saw a large picture of myself, a banner really, hanging from the side of a condo tower. Under my face were the following words:

WE ARE NAKED AS THE NIGHT.

WE ARE NAKED IN THIS FIGHT.

I'm not sure what those words and my face had to do with each other, but I was glad in their use.

I was about to walk up to another of my fellow naked riders and ask about the banner when another hand clamped down on my shoulder.


Suddenly, I was clothed and sitting in the passenger seat of a large SUV. Looking out the window, all I could make out through the harsh red glare was a wasteland of sand and downed buildings, power lines, and trees.

That's when a blue-haired woman in a flak jacket said, "Hold on to your butt. It gets rough about here."

Before I could respond to that, I had to grab for the "Oh shit!" handles. I clenched my eyes and held on tight. I don't think that I'd ever been on a roller coaster with as many sharp turns, changes in speed, and drops. Oh, the drop.

I wanted to keep my eyes closed tight, but I forced them open anyway. I didn't know what could happen to me here. Everything felt real, so I guess I was still afraid that I would feel some horrible pain if we crashed. I felt every jarring bounce, so other, worse pain, didn't seem out of the realm of possibility.

When I got my eyes open, I wished I'd kept them closed.

We were quickly approaching a ledge. It was as if we were in one of Ken Avidor's apocalyptic cartoon visions of the Twin Cities. What must have been the 94 bridge over the Mississippi River looked as if some great lizard from the watery depth had taken a bite out of it. Despite the bridge's dilapidation, we were not slowing.

I squeaked, "Stop."

"What?" She saw me pointing out the window. "Oh, yeah. Don't worry. We're fine." And she stomped on the gas, sending us speeding over the edge.

The SUV hung in the air longer than I had expected. Hanging there, out over the Mississippi River, somehow gave me a new respect for Michael Jordan's feats of athleticism. However, we couldn't stay aloft forever. Perhaps minutes went by, or fear lengthened those seconds, but we started to drop. First, the nose of the SUV, heavier than the rear, tipped forward. I caught a good view of the slowly drifting watery expanse that would be my final resting place—again, being dead did not, for some reason, mean that I had lost my self-preservation instincts.

I must have been screaming. The blue-haired woman had let go of the steering wheel and was trying to calm me down. Her method was not the most caring. But before I could object to her punching me in the arm, we hit the water.

Safely through, we'd landed on all four wheels. When I looked around, we were under the Mississippi River. The walls around us were white stone and unfinished. I was trying to make out the rest of the strange room, including what looked like Batman's secret cave: one entire wall was dedicated to a projector screen that flickered with statistics like the stock exchange.

I'd been smuggled out of one dream and into another. In this dream, there was a resistance, and I was in a truck with its leader. However, unlike the nudist critical mass trying to save Minneapolis from cars, I had no idea what was being protested or resisted here.

"We have to talk."

I turned to the blue-haired woman. I don't like to think I behave according to hormones, but she stirred up a storm in me that caused my eyes to roam her body. I lingered over one of her tattoos, an *Earth First!* logo graced the underside of her arm. I had an odd feeling about this woman, a feeling that kept me quiet and hopeful.

"Stop raping me with your eyes. I'm up here." She pointed to her eyes. "Here." Then she continued, "We don't have much time. They'll take you back again soon, so just listen."

I nodded.

"You're going to be given a choice. You are going to have to choose between futures. Why you are going to be given the opportunity to direct the future, I can't answer. Perhaps, you did something honorable or of note. I don't know, and I don't care. What matters is that you are going to decide where we go from here.

"I yanked you from one future, but I think this game is shit. I was like you, once. I was given a choice, but I couldn't choose. Now, it's all about you. You are the key to the future. It is your choice. However, all of your choices are false. Each one is flawed. Trust me. Even if they look idyllic, they are not. Some flaw will present itself."

I interrupted, "I think that I was starting to see the flaw when you pulled me into your SUV. I don't know if I can articulate what was wrong, but something was definitely not right."

"Good. I knew you'd be able to see. Anyway, you'll have to choose between three bad choices. I don't know why they all have a rotten core, but they do. When making your choice, you need to make sure that you've seen the rotten core. Make sure that you know what horror you are choosing for the living. I can't tell you what to choose, but you'll know what to do when the time comes."

Lines formed around her mouth and eyes. She said, "You're starting to rust. Our time is up."

I quickly looked at my hands, which were turning reddish brown and starting to flake. Just as I started to panic, I was back on my bike, naked. The transition was worse than the drop into the Mississippi River, and I emptied the contents of my stomach. When I was done, I looked at my hands, my legs, and they were clear. There was no sign of the red flakes I'd just glimpsed.

"I thought I'd lost you," said the black man who'd started me down this magic carpet ride. "You alright there?" he asked, finally noticing that I was doubled over and dry heaving. "Call me Ken, anyway."

I'm not sure what was more startling that he didn't know I'd been gone or that he'd chosen that specific moment to introduce himself. Either way, thinking about his name, Ken, stopped my convolutions, and I was grateful. Then, I remembered, rotten core.

I looked around as if out of the corner of my eye some visual representation of the decrepit would present itself. I didn't even know what I was going to see. It wasn't as if evil was going to simply walk up and introduce itself. In my experience, evil wore a spandex racing suit and claimed to represent my best interests while telling me to be calm and work with the system instead of against it. I thought I had a handle on this one.

"Ken," I asked, "What is this rally going to achieve?" I didn't expect a straight answer. I expected Ken to give me some Popsicle of a line that would taste good but leave my hand and mouth sticky.

Instead, Ken said, "We're not here for the rally, silly. You're here to see the end of your legacy." He shrugged. "It was a good run you know. Minneapolis was a North Star, a hope in the darkness that humanity would one day depart from automobile use. But, all dreams come to an end." He pointed, "Look."

I watched as a parade of paddy wagons and black trucks with "S.W.A.T." written in white across the side rolled up to the intersection. Men with guns, riot shields, batons, and gas grenades funneled out of the trucks into a semicircle separating bystanders and the nudist cyclers.

One shout led to chanting, which led to gas, which led to shooting. I ducked just in time, as bullets whizzed by me. When the shooting was over, I left Ken's side and walked through the carnage of bleeding nudes twisted up with bike frames and tires to stand beside a young boy.

The boy couldn't have been more than eight or nine years old. He was nude and stood beside a tricked out Mongoose dirt bike. He'd been shot and was bleeding from a wound in his right leg. He stood strong as he dipped his finger into his open wound to finish writing something on the condo wall in blood where the banner of my face had hung only minutes ago. He wrote: SEWARD'S LAST STAND.

Bravado not withstanding, I'd had enough of these spiritual jump-cuts and juxtapositions.

A lovely couple, mid twenties, obviously in love by the way they walked hand-in-hand, lockstep, stopped at an unknown intersection and kissed. I longed, just for a moment, for a hippy chick I'd known once. We were free with the love, not a care in the world, except for the explorations of each other's body. There had been no end to our explorations, a youthful freedom of curves, fingers, fluids, lips, and skin. But, as I'd heard recently, all dreams come to an end. So too did the lights change, causing the young lovers to quickly cross the street. The woman running ahead, her hand still caught in his. She was forced to turn around, arm out stretched with a broad laughing smile. He hurried up, scooped her in his arms and carried her the rest of the way across the street, nuzzling noses.

I was alone to wander, to see what I could peel back from the edges of this sequence of events. And in a moment when I'd about given up on clues to where or when I was, I saw what looked like Pugsley's fat-tired bike from which he derived his alias. If it wasn't his bike, it was a damn fine copy. I scanned around—no one. The only people I'd seen were the laughing lovers hours ago. Seeing a replica of Pugsley's bike, I felt like I'd stumbled upon some tool left by the gods. Well, I wasn't going to pass it up. I rolled it back from the bike rack and rode down the street. I stopped at the corner and looked back. *Nope. No one was chasing me,* so I decided that either the gods were looking out for me or if not the gods, Pugsley himself.

Other than the distinct absence of people, I could have been in my own time on any block in Minneapolis or St. Paul that I'd not had the chance to explore. The leaves were turning from deep green to shades of red and yellow. I passed an ash tree that had started to blaze a fire red. A few leaves were being tossed about by dust devils. The light slanted from the south and west meaning it would be dark soon. Still, no people were on the streets.

Finally, I spotted a familiar landmark, the state fairgrounds. I was in St. Paul. "Crap," I was in St. Paul. *What the hell am I doing in St. Paul?* I have nothing against St. Paul. St. Paul is a happening place, what with the Xcel Energy Center and all. I just knew Minneapolis better. Minneapolis is like the dirty baseball cap that your lover has asked you to toss, but you just can't part with.

A large hillbilly short-bed pickup with roll bars and balloon tires pulled up to gate ahead of me. Four large fellas practically fell out of the back carrying shotguns and sporting machetes. They looked right at me.

"You," called the one in overalls. "Who let you out?"

"I was never in."

They laughed. Some joke that I was not privy too. However, they stopped laughing when I presumed to ride on down the road.

"Stop."

I wasn't inclined to stick around. I didn't like the look of these folks. I'm not one to judge looks, but they did not look like they wanted me over for pizza and a beer. I pedaled faster.

Boom! A shot fired.

I straddled the Pugsley with my hands in the air.

Then, I was ripped from the bike and tossed to the ground. A heavy knee was pressed into my back as my hands were tethered. I tried to tune out their witty banter about "hogtied" and "got you now," but I couldn't.

"What we got us here?"

"Looks like one of those bicycle freaks out of Minneapolis."

"You know the deal. We don't cross the river, and they don't cross the river."

"Well, he crossed the river."

"Point."

"Damn straight, point."

One of them, I'm assuming the one who'd last spoke, to punctuate his point, shot his gun in the air. Well, I hoped it was in the air.

"So, we can eat 'em then."

"He does look ripe, damn near plump in the middle."

One of them kicked me, hard, in the side. I tried to roll, but someone was still holding me down with his knee. All I could do was groan and try to shift my weight. I knew one of them had said eat. I still wasn't sure they meant any of it, and I wasn't positive I'd be around when the cooking started if they were serious. Who knew, I could be off somewhere else at any minute. I wanted to be. *Fuck.* I should have walked through the door of light Pugsley Henderson had offered. I should be walking the aisles of the big bike junkyard in the sky. But no, I had to be stubborn and see. *See what?* See that the world is as fucked up as I thought it was? I should be covered in holy chain grease, truing halos and tires for the crew.

"Yup. He's looking tasty."

"Toss his sweet ass in with the others then."


Admitting I am wrong about some historical fact or whatever is one thing, but having to admit that they were going to eventually eat me was entirely another. I was in what could only be described as a corral for cattle, except instead of cows, or even horses, there were about thirty other people. So far, as if for protection, the others steered clear of me.

Not knowing how much time I'd have here, I needed to get to the bottom of this reality. I needed to see what was right because being locked up with the threat of being eaten was definitely what was wrong. *Where was the hope?* The hope in the last vision was that the nude protestors would serve as some type of group-martyr, like the World Trade Organization riots in Seattle, WA. Once news of the violence spread, I was sure awareness would spread and something would change. Change is the constant after all.

I was still deep in thought when a woman with tea cup sized breasts and green eyes along with a man with little muscle definition and a full beard approached me.

The woman held out her hand. I took it.

"Irene." She let go and backed out of the man's way.

"A pleasure."

The man stepped forward and stood between us. He didn't say a word and kept his eyes on the ground.

Irene said, "They are going to eat you."

"I figured."

"Thank you." She pointed to the man between us. "He was up for dinner tonight before you came along. They like fresh meat, so they won't let you fester long."

I nodded. "What is this place?"

She shook her head. "I don't know. I've been here maybe

two weeks, but I still don't know. I was on my way north to Stillwater. I was going to see family and go boating on the St. Croix, but I crashed my car. Now that I think of it, I'm sure it was a trap." She balled her fists. "Whatever this place is, I know it won't last long. People can't eat people and get away with it. It's not right."

"So," I eased into it, "this is the only cannibalism camp you've seen?"

"Well, no." She turned to look over at the others. "And, yes. I've never seen one, but I've heard that they've been popping up all over the States. I just didn't believe the news. Something in the drinking water, I guess. Over exposure to what causes a living form of Zombie-ism."

I tried not to laugh. I was on the menu for tonight, and it looked like she believed what she was saying. "Sorry. I guess I don't get out much. I'm kind of a loner, no TV, no radio. I just keep to myself, mostly."

She nodded and accepted my lie. "The first case was reported about five years ago in Cleveland. It was written off as some new cult. Then nothing. Now…" She looked at the ground. "I'm sorry, but they're here."

I turned to see a different group of men. These men were dressed in culinary uniforms, baggy checkered pants and white—blood stained—chef's coats. Each wielded a long, sharp-looking knife. Confident that I'd be whisked away before any real danger threatened my person, I walked away from Irene and over to the cooks.

"Told you," said one, "he's a bold one, likely to be tasty."

"Shut up."

They took me out of the pen. Perhaps because I didn't put up a fight, they didn't bind my hands again. Instead, they were content to allow me to walk among them. We turned down Johnson Street toward where, if the fair were up and running, the fancy chickens would have been shown.

When we got to another barn, they pushed me inside. The scene was horrific and turned my stomach. The killing floor was a sloppy mess of blood, hair, and piles of skin. Two large hooks hung from the ceiling over several white buckets used to catch and collect blood. A couple of the buckets were full.

Suddenly, the hooks dropped to the floor where one of the cooks stood. He picked them up and clanged them together. The sound sent shivers through my body. As I was marched over to the hooks, I kept looking around, waiting for something to happen, waiting to be whisked away. I had a larger fate waiting for me elsewhere, or so I had convinced myself.

Then it was dark.

Throbbing, all I could feel was a dull but all-consuming headache. When I managed to open my eyes, I could see the ground beneath me, only inches away. I could make out laughing in the background, but I couldn't change my position to see what was going on. My only view was of the blood buckets below me, and the steady drip coming from my throat. I'd seen organic free-range chickens bled, so I knew I didn't have long. I admitted my mistake. I should have fought. I shouldn't have believed I'd be stolen from this dream at the last minute to some other hell. What difference did it make anyway, this hellish ending or another? Everything ends. If I couldn't work on bikes and feel the wind in my hair as I rode down The Greenway, this end was as good as any other. At least I'd given Irene's friend another day.

Strange, but as I hung there, I noticed that my arms were starting to flake small metallic looking chips. Then it was dark, again.


Listless, I tried to move and found that I could. I let out a deep sigh that shook my gut. It felt good. I was, well, "alive" was the wrong word. Perhaps, "still" is the word I needed. Before opening my eyes to see what new terror awaited me, I pondered the blue-haired woman's words.

If she knew anything at all, I was going to have to choose between horrors. Could I choose cannibalism?


Minneapolis, through a treaty was a ward of Canada while St. Paul remained in the U.S. Strangely, those on the St. Paul side, who once would have never considered even a day trip into Minneapolis, were desperate to cross the wall.

I spent years here. I had needed to set up shop again to feed my hungry stomach. It was as if everything up until the moment I landed on the Minneapolis side, in Loring Park, had been the dream of my homeless-self. Homelessness is no joke especially when you believe you're dead and viewing society as a ghost drifting by like some cotton candy cloud. After a couple of days of sleeping where my head fell and going hungry, I made the decision to make the best of my new home.

I started by collecting junk bikes. I knew bikes, and there were enough of them lying around unattended that I could begin a type of salvage. Without tools and a space to work, I piled my finds under the 94 overpass near the Lyndale Historical Farmer's Market. No one cared. The bikes were crap, bent to hell and worthless to anyone else.

After a while, I had a mountain of scrap. I'd even come across some crude stripped out tools. From the scrap pile, I constructed a dozen usable bikes. Happily, and even though I didn't recognize this era's hipsters, single speed bikes were still all the rage. In a town with a seemingly eternal winter, less was more. I was able to sell them all and buy a year's use of a storage unit. Home. Workshop. I made the storage unit work. I even had enough money left to buy a good set of wrenches and a multi-tool.

I thought that I was doing fairly well. I really didn't have much time to think about the politics of the time or why more and more of the Minneapolis population was beginning to speak a strange hybridized version of French. I was bone thin and happy. I had a roof, food, and a purpose. I didn't even think back on the dream much anymore, except for this strange rust colored skin irritation developing around my knees and elbows. I simply lived day-by-day, a routine of bike sales and scavenging for parts and food. Then, I met Fredrick.

Fredrick was young and in love. His high school lover had been on the St. Paul side when the wall went up. But, Fredrick convinced me, enlisted me really, in his plan to smuggle his lover, Hanna, into Minneapolis.

"Why not get yourself into St. Paul?" I asked as we sat around a barrel fire. I was homeless. He was not. Fredrick liked to slum with us because he felt we were real. None of us minded because he always brought food. Tonight, he had brought with him twelve large pizzas. He was a good kid, a bit aimless, but good. He stood about five-seven and couldn't grow whiskers if his life depended on it. He had long hair that he usually let fall over his face. He didn't look like he got much sun, but since the war with Canada, the sky was rarely clear. "I hear people are trying to get into Minneapolis, but they aren't trying to get into St. Paul. I bet you could slip in and no one would care."

He moped and kicked an empty can of black beans. "True."

"Good."

"I want her here. Here, we could marry and have kids without having to worry about health care costs."

"Health care?"

"Yeah." He looked at me—my shabby shoes, pants with holes, and layers of decomposing shirts. "Well. You do know that you're entitled to housing assistance and job placement if you are able. Oh, and if you not able, you're entitled to other types of assistance."

I eyed him. I didn't know what to say other than I didn't

know that I was entitled to anything. I guess I was still operating under the assumption that I was in America and in America, you're entitled to shit. In the America I knew, everyone worked and either succeeded or failed. I was starting to succeed and to know that I could have had help left a bitter taste in my mouth. Yes, I wanted help. I was hungry all the time. Why hadn't anyone told me there was a way into a real bed? All I could bring myself to say was, "You're kidding, right?"

"No, the Office of the Under Privileged works with the homeless to help them find work, food, and a living space. They could even help you with that rash." He pointed to my cheeks that were, admittedly, beginning to flake. "Here in Canada, no one needs go it alone. Which is why I can't stand the thought of Hanna over there in America. By now, she'd be starving like you, and being a woman…"

He didn't want to say it, but I knew he was thinking that she'd be forced into the sex trade. An attractive teenage girl would bring top dollar. I took another bite of pizza and patted him on the shoulder. "How much do you love her?"

"I'd do anything."

Well, I was sold and a sucker. I was going to help Fredrick smuggle Hanna into Canadian-Minneapolis. While I was at it, I was going to have him show me where this magical Office of the Under Privileged was located.


While standing in line at the Office of the Under Privileged, which was indeed just as magical as Fredrick said, I helped him draw up plans to rescue Hanna from the clutches of the American sex trade. The line was long. Apparently, quite a number of people felt under privileged. However, it was made clear that I needed the longest line of them all. I was in the line with the other ex-American homeless with no I.D.

Fredrick had a map. He'd already scouted the wall and determined a weak spot near the University of Minnesota, now known as the University of Southern Canada, lovingly referred to as the Loonies. Fredrick was certain that there were tunnels, old ones, which ran under the university and under the wall. He said that St. Paul never bothered to rebuild because the majority of the academics ended up on the Canadian side.

While we discussed how to enter those old tunnels and Fredrick's lack of success as a writer, I managed to make it to the front of the line.

"I.D.?" asked a hollow-eyed government clerk. She had round cheeks that were losing their rosiness and eyes that wanted something to sparkle about but could find nothing. Her hair was short and as black as her mascara. She repeated, "I.D.?"

"No. Sorry, I don't have an I.D." I said trying to be cheery. I wanted to see her eyes sparkle. I wanted her cheeks to be rosy.

"Of course you don't," she said, "you're in the line for ex-Americans without identification." She swiveled a screen so that she and I could both see it. "Name?"

"Daniel Seward."

"Date of birth?"

"1962."

She stopped typing and looked at me. If there were ever going to be sparkles in those eyes of hers, I'd just ruined any chance of them appearing today.

"I think you need a different line." She pointed to a window down the hall. There was no one in line at the new window. "Please, sir, umm…Mr. Seward, step out of line. You are at the wrong window." Then, she closed her window.

Fredrick was still standing next to me, but must not have heard anything that I'd said to the government clerk. He was still studying the maps and drawings of the old University of Minnesota. So, I walked over to interrupt his meditations.

"I need a different window." I pointed down the hall.

He shrugged his shoulders, "At least the line's short. I'll take a seat over there." Fredrick pointed to a row of brown chairs near a TV screen. He wandered off, his nose in his maps.

Despite having wasted half the day in the wrong line, I was still in a good mood. I didn't expect getting the type of help the Office of the Under Privileged offered was going to be as simple as, "How do you do?" So, I knocked at the closed window, which had a sign taped to it that read, PLEASE KNOCK.

The window opened almost at once. On the other side of the window sat the same small woman who'd recommended this window over the previous one. This time she just started in with the questions rather than attempt to open with a joke.

"Name?"

"Daniel Seward."

"Date of birth?"

"1962."

"Is that rust on your cheeks?"

I brushed my cheek and a few stiff flakes fell onto the counter. "Rust?"

"That's what I thought." She pushed a small yellow button, which in retrospect should have been red. It was the type of button that should have had a stronger color than yellow. Yellow is not the color I'd associate with large men in white coats wielding needles.


"Decide."

When I had woken, I felt strange and the room was blurry. I felt the urge to empty my stomach, like I'd just woken from dental surgery. Except at the dentist, I hadn't been tied to the chair and was able to turn my head and puke on the floor. Here, I had no choice.

"Decide."

There it was again. A voice, deep and guttural, which I believed came from just beyond the light aiming right into my eyes.

"Decide."

This must be the moment, the moment that the girl with the blue-hair had spoken about, warned me was coming.

"Decide."

"Okay. Okay. Just a minute."

"Decide."

"Just a minute." I waited. Nothing. I guessed that I was being given my minute. I thought about the three options. None appealed to me in the way that I'd hoped, and I really hadn't had the time to get a good feeling for any of them. Well, I guess if I'd stayed at the fairgrounds, I'd have been eaten. If I'd stayed with the nudist bikers, I'd be dead or living in a world that was about to fall apart. The only one that I'd had anytime to really get to know was the last, and it seemed too good to be true.

I wondered how Fredrik was getting along. I sure did hope that he'd found others to help rescue Hanna from the American sex trade in St. Paul. He did seem to love her and want the best for her.

"Decide."

My minute was up. The blue-haired girl had been right. All my choices were bad choices. I had to pick the one in which I hadn't seen the good yet, like the teenagers I helped while I was alive. Surly, something good must come. So I said, "Option B."

"It was your choice," the voice said matter-of-factly, "and you chose B."

Pugsley stood next to me shaking his head. "Man, I hope all that nonsense was worth it to you."

We were somewhere dark. I could see his face and his hands. When I raised my own hands, I could see that they were a flaky mess. I was even missing my ring finger and thumb on my right hand.

"Are you ready?" He asked me.

A hallway illuminated. It was long and I couldn't see where it went. Then, there was a bike resting next to me. It was my bike, my semi-recumbent cruiser. When I inspected the cruiser more closely, it too was covered in some type of flaky corrosion. I gripped the handlebars, and they crumbled.

I asked, "What's going on?"

"The rust, it got you." He shook his head. "You've over-spent your stay, man."


The blue-haired girl's jaw hung wide open. "So, let me get this straight. You chose hillbilly cannibal rednecks over an auto-mobile free Minneapolis and a Minneapolis that had been an-nexed by Canada."

"It seemed the truest. I'm not a hero, and I can't imagine Minneapolis ever being completely free from cars. Besides, that dream had already come to an end. Cars were being let back in."

"You don't know that. Perhaps, the deaths of the nude rid-ers would have made a difference."

"When have protests of that nature ever changed anything? And Canada? Really, I'm a patriot at heart. I couldn't allow it."

She spat at me. "You don't come back from the rust, you know. You end up..." she shrugged, "...nothing." Then, she kicked dirt in my face.

I watched her walk away and get into her SUV and drive off. I could do nothing more than watch. My legs had separated from my torso. Leaning against a tree was all I could do to remain upright.

She was wrong about the rust, Pugsley too. When rain began to fall, I thought that was it for me. Each drop that hit me exploded. I lost huge sections of my body until I was nothing more than a muddy puddle of dust beneath the tree. It would have been better if they were right, and I would have ceased to exist.

Instead, I float upon the breeze, witness to horrors I so boldly chose for humanity, waiting. Waiting for the good I believe follows every storm, a rainbow in the night.

# The Man with Two Hearts In His Ribcage

## By Max Hrabal

Naked to his drawers Hunson Caffrey sat windowside of the double looking down many stories. A billion cubic inches of smog air held up by lights, all the colors down there fluttering and hugging brown outlines. In his hands turned a card printed with an address in Tianjin. The name and title he'd long scraped away: Hanta Meyrink, Surgeon, Open Heart Services. He might have memorized the address, but it was Chinese.

He checked his hung clothes again. Shirt mostly dry. Pants, vest and jacket wet, smelling like hotel shampoo and whatever was in the water. The door opened and the roommate, a Californian, walked through it, throwing his key card by the TV. He oohed and ahhed. Hunson took down the shirt and pulled it on, buttoning from the bottom.

"Helluva scar," the roommate said. "War?

Hunson grunted, faced the window. He had cut the sutures out two weeks before.

"You poor bastards. All I got was the clap." He lay out on his unmade bed and lit a cigarette. Hunson felt the pants again. Wool dries slow, he thought.

"Don't you have any other clothes in that suitcase, brother? Don't tell me you're that broke."

Hunson told him nothing. The suitcase at the foot of his bed was full of cardboard and a cinderblock and it was locked.

"Dinner's in an hour," the roommate talked to the ceiling and his voice bounced off it. "Can't wait to meet the wives. I got mine all picked out. I figure no one'll want her cause she's got a lazy eye. But she's loaded. And she looks alright from the pictures. Besides," he inhaled smoke deeply," even the rich ones here'll cook and clean." He propped himself on an elbow and ashed the cigarette. "We got free time til then, you wanna fool around?"

Hunson touched the pants again. The crotch was dry at least. He took the pants down and stepped into them, tucking in his shirt and sliding the card into the breast pocket.


She found him at the end of the buffet line.

"You are from the middle west of America." She touched the Chinese writing on his nametag and left her finger there. "What city?"

"Twin Cities," he told her, a full plate of food in one hand.

"From two cities?"

"Yes," he said. "We just call it that."

"I like America."

"Me too," he read the English on her nametag: Zhang, Shirley Temple. She wore a long dress covered in symbols.

"I think we can talk more," she said. "Shall we eat together?"

"Ok." He nodded and she led him to a table. They passed the Californian and the woman with the lazy eye. Seated, he began eating. Noodles, oil, meat. Shirley leaned on the table. She had no plate.

"I have seen your profile images," she said. "You were a soldier."

He would not claim that. "I drove a truck," he said. If she was disappointed it did not show.

"What have you been doing with yourself afterwards."

He had early on determined not to lie, to keep things simple. But he left much out. "I finished school. And I was asked to join a committee. To work on the treaty." It was not the whole truth, he had turned the job down.

"Chairman?"

"Sub-chair."

"I don't like politics."

"Me neither."

The other women and men stood or sat around the tables in groups and pairs. There were aggressive men, talking to three women at once. Others sat alone drinking the free booze and waiting.

She saw him looking around. "You don't like whiskey?"

"No," he touched his chest. "Not anymore."

"That's good. Good for your body."

"Listen, ma'm, have you ever been to Tianjin?"

"Yes," she said and her eyelids fluttered, "it is very close."

He knew that. "How much for a ticket?"

"You want to go there?"

"Maybe."

"You had better not go there. Here is better."

"Ok." He dropped it.

"Is it as bad as they say in America?"

"It's been worse."

At the club the women paid for everything. Hunson drank tonic water and sat with Shirley by the wall. She said it was noisy. The lasers and smoke made his eyes water. When he left she followed him out.

In her room at the hotel, a single in another wing, more finely furnished and larger than his room, she touched the scar. He lay sweating and his overpacked chest heaved in quadruple beats. Too much strain, he thought. No way around it.

"It was a bad war," she whispered, ear to the pillow, hand lingering on the white and purple seam of skin that rose and fell. "You lost your friends."

His breathing slowed. Cloudbursts over new deserts. Tanks scoring the cobblestones of Ljubliana, megaphone echoes, anthems, lost in the disintegrate air. Soundwaves scattered on bosonic winds. Thought ripped into constituent energy running away.

"My brother." His pulse slowed. It calmed him to say it. Like at the hospital in Lagos going under, on a table by his brother. Him to return and his brother not to, but for the heart that lingered now knit to Hunson's own. The pain eased, part of it, and he slept.

Water running, a shower. Distant morning sounds of traffic on the window pane. On the bed table he found his clothes, folded. Blinking sleep away he checked the pocket of his shirt. The card was there, a sheaf of international credit bills behind it. And a note in delicate hand. "Enough for Tianjin." He dressed and walked out of the room, took the elevator to one, and left the hotel.


From the belly of the train he watched hoops and streamers of light distend in the murk and speed. Cities running together. Tianjin was the same, but browner, darker. Like Lagos, like Amman. He thought of driving under clear skies in Cameroon, Algeria, the battle continent. The Mississippi. Clouds that stayed where they belonged.

In the watery street, muffled foghorns blasted from afar,

dynamoes hummed on skyways above, propelling straight trucks, tractor-trailers, busses and firefly cabs. Trains coupled clanging from the station. Sweating and stinking he climbed into a taxi and showed the driver his destination.

His eyes opened wide for one gasping look onto a dreamworld that was the real world. The way fish see the dry world when we pull them out. A man in white without a face held two hearts over him, in each latex hand he lifted one then the other, taking stock of their heft and quality. Like newborn babes or nuggets of precious ore, they were. "Just one," he tried to say, jawing the numb air with his mind. Tubes ran from his chest to the floor, the walls. His lungs were still and he saw the inner wall of his ribcage laid open. Blood entered in jerks and twitches, mechanical clicks carried in the fluid of his capillaries and found the hearing part of his brain before he fell away again.

He came to over weeks. And when he could stand he walked from the sickbed to the bank and presently held newly minted cash in his pocket. The bills bore a likeness of the round rough globe and he ran his thumb over the moutains and coastlines. Outside the bank a woman sold flowers from an electric rickshaw. He bought a white one and fed the stem through his lapel while she went to make change. In an underpass he found a barber and sat in the rumbling shade to have his face scraped clean. He walked all day, pale and thin and eating everything, stopping to watch men fish the canal with long poles. He looked for the ocean, but could not find it. The next day he boarded a train back to Beijing.

He looked for her, but the profile was gone. No record of her passing through the marriage service. An English-speaking tech in a wire-cluttered warren told him it was no use trying to find her by that name. It only dragged up old pictures and clips of a long dead child entertainer, he said, from America's frontier days. When Hunson refused to pay, two men appeared and beat the cash from him.

He returned to the hotel late and limping and the lounge was empty but for the Black African who dealt cards there. The man watched Hunson cross the lobby and board the glass elevator. As it ascended he watched the man's head crane up, until Hunson rose so high he could no longer distinguish the green felt card table from the other tables and potted plants so far below.

The sun was yellow and insubstantial through the branches, giving little light, but much heat. Women danced circles around the park rotunda to a music half played, half programmed. The other man on the bench spoke London English with a Slavic accent, dropping Ts and rolling Rs. He spoke like a man who felt his time was often wasted.

"If you don't mind my asking, what is it you want with her?"

"I want to contact her. I owe her some money."

"Now if you don't mind my asking another, what line of work are you in?"

"I'm living on an inheritance. But I was in the service."

"Now I know why you came to us, but this is not precisely the kind of work we normally do, you understand?"

"The Refugee Services Bureau recommended you for missing people."

"I get that my friend, and 'missing persons' for us generally means refugees, the diaspora. Reuniting families and that. And you have given me the impression that this woman is not in fact missing, but rather that you don't happen to know where she is, which is more than likely right where she belongs."

"You can't do it."

"I didn't say that. I'll put the Chinese boys on it. But don't get your hopes up is all. Take my card here. You have a card? You don't have a card."

"I'm staying at the Rainbird. I'll let you know if I move."

The hotel served trust fund refugees, investors, pensioned veterans, war profiteers, and all drank together nightly in the lounge. He avoided them and spent long hours alone on the hotel room console. When his eyes went sore he sought wealthy Chinese men named Zhang and asked after their daughters. Some said they had some, but not of that name, others laughed, and others offered to arrange introductions. When he walked in the city many people spat when they saw him and as many shook his hand or tried to hug him. He found himself in unprovoked conversations touching on the vaguaries of death, loss, forgiveness and reconciliation. Most ignored him. He returned nightly to invisible hands groping inside his chest or a heart floating above his bed, tethered to his ribs like a balloon.

In a poor quarter on the south fourth ring he found the place described to him, a dog skin stretched over an archway and a courtyard of dirt within. A large boy of seventeen or more with dark skin squatted on a plastic stool drinking soup. The boy looked at him, then all but drained his bowl and stood to cast the dregs into the dirt. He led Hunson to a shack of styrofoam and old tabletops with many sheets of tarpaulin hung to make a door. Inside he motioned him to sit on a stool and said in broken English that he would need money before he woke his grandmother to come and speak, but gave no price. Hunson produced several bills and the boy took them and went out. A tin lamp smoked on the floor and smelled like burning crude. A table set with small glasses and a bottle of clear liquor before a small shrine of bone and ribbon was the only other furnishing.

He waited a long time before the boy returned holding an old woman tightly before him. The two were bound together at wrist and knee and the boy half squatted as he walked to the shrine, moving the limbs of the old limp woman, pushing his stomach into her back and kicking their legs together forward as her puppeteer. Her head lolled back on his shoulder, eyes rolling with his chin forward on hers. The boy guided the woman's hands to the bottle and they came alive, encircling the glasses and pouring out full measures in each, swinging the right arms around to Hunson. He took it and they drank together, the boy watching her mouth carefully as he helped her pour the flaming liquid down. Then the old woman took up a wailing and moaning and the pair swayed together and shook and jumped as though dancing against their will to unheard music. It lasted long and she cut her ululations short only to draw breath. Hunson sat and watched all this. When finally it stopped the boy untied the woman, easing her to the dirt floor to gasp. The boy's shirt and pantfronts were wet with their mingled sweat.

The boy stood and rubbed his wrists and told Hunson what had happened and how it had. That she had seen his brother and had been his brother, and his brother was full of color from the other world which was good, and that his brother wished to tell him they were together now and would be also in the next world and be there in peace, and that the one who carried his brother's heart now was a person who had been given another chance in a world of few second chances. When he asked about Shirley, the boy nodded and told him the spirits only offer as much as they are inclined to give and always mysteriously, but that she had not yet crossed into the other world. Hunson paid again for their ancestors' spirits and his own and left the young man to care for his drained and shaken elder. Outside the moon was up and he picked his way through the yard to find the road again.

At the hotel he found the card dealer sitting alone as was his late-night habit and he called to Hunson with a laugh and an unintelligible word, for his accent was strange. Hunson approached and sat at the fan-shaped card table.

"You have been out late again," he said. "We are two night owls, you and me. Two men with wide eyes that can see in the night."

"I guess we are." A waiter appeared and Hunson ordered water and asked to buy the man's beer. The waiter left and returned with the drinks and left again. "I sometimes see you watching me."

The man spoke and Hunson rested and listened and was told the story of the man's life. He was half-Chinese, he said. A wanderer, he claimed, and a time-traveller, and never took the title of refugee though others wore it proudly, but Hunson thought the man still was. He had been a student of wind technology when the war came to his West African city. He was groomed like his father and his father's father to work in the ranks of the Zhang Power Cooperative. It was this name Zhang, of course, that kept Hunson that night at the man's table. He had been to banquets and ceremonies and seen the trustees all together and drank with them and met their daughters. But he had lost his mind in the war and when it ended there was no school and no job, no Zhangs in Africa anymore. So he left for Beijing to find his piece of the empire promised to him since those early days and somehow came to shuffle cards for the hotel's take, like a gypsy, working for the kinds of men he once thought he could become.

"We are the same," he told Hunson. "In that we carry traded burdens. Mine of a full mind and yours of a full heart." Hunson nodded and did not know fully what he meant but knew that it was true.

"There are madmen who don't know they're mad and carry sanity insanely. But men like us know better. We are the same. Even now the forests we, you and I, saw burned up, are returning and no one thinks they have the time to watch them grow." He pushed the cards around on the felt with gloved hands, flipping and arranging them as though they told the same thing as his words and he was merely reading what they said.

"You fought in the war," said Hunson.

He shuffled quietly, looking for a way to speak to the matter. "When you stand on the traffic median between two opposing lanes, can you claim to go one way or the other? No. You can either wait for it to ebb and cross then, or else for someone to stop and pick you up, but the greater flow will never stop. This is where we stand in time."

Hunson considered this. "We might stay out of it."

"Though we might try, we will always hear it roaring in the

distance, if only in our dreams, and this is war." They sat in silence for some time until Hunson left his glass full of water and wished the man good night.

He slept well and in the morning called the office of the missing persons service. He was told the number had changed, the service closed. He asked the woman on the other end for some further explanation, but she offered only that these were hectic times, and then apologized.


In the mirror he pulled up the top stitch and slid one scissor-blade under along the skin, snipping it and pulling the smooth black thread by the knot through its tunnel in the scar. Scar on scar. One by one he drew them out. When he was finished he threw the tangle in a bin beside the sink and brushed flakes of dried skin and pus away, wiping the ridges and furrows clean.

# Wardrobe Malfunction
## By Dale Newton

Amy could just kick herself for forgetting to charge her blouse. Now she wouldn't be able to set it to that confident maroon color for the job interview this morning. Instead the blouse displayed the checkerboard default pattern that was supposed to remind her to charge it up. Of course, it ran out of power while she slept last night, so today she would show up for the interview looking like the winner's flag at the Daytona Electric 500. She had adjusted her skirt color to warning-flag yellow in an attempt to make it look like a fashion choice.

At least, it was clean . . . *Damn!* It wasn't even that. The auto clean died with the color. So now she was wearing a dirty winner's flag to the first meeting with her (hopefully) future boss.

She would have to make the best of it. She couldn't afford to buy a new blouse on her current salary, and her other blouse was in the shop for repairs. That one started blinking transparent while she presented her report on the ridership levels for the central-corridor bike highway between Minneapolis and St. Paul. Good thing she'd worn an opaque bra that day. Maybe the undergarment's pattern of retro Michelle Obama campaign images had won her some points with the liberals on the legislative committee. There were certainly smiles from all of those grey-haired boys at the time. After that fiasco, she had changed the setting on this blouse from transparent to a checkerboard as its default. The unplanned checkerboard pattern was better than showing up in the Emperor's new clothes for today's interview.

A push of wind announced the arrival of the Metropolitan Levtran at the platform, and all the waiting commuters shifted their weight in readiness to flow onboard. She hardly had to move a muscle to be carried along with the crowd as it stepped forward through the opening doors as if controlled by a hive mind. Being near the front of the platform, she was able to occupy one of the few remaining seats in the passenger car she'd entered. It wasn't an ideal seat. A teenage boy was standing directly in front of her, affording her an eye-level view of his long underwear, which was presenting realistic floating images of cuts of meat. It was a backside view, at that. Around his ankles was the obligatory suggestion of denim jeans, really just an oddly shaped denim belt. In an emergency, he might be able to take a half step before he fell and was trampled by the panicked crowd, Amy decided. As if in response to her unsympathetic prediction, the young man changed his standing positions to give her a close view of the front side of the digital long johns. She looked away, pretending to be reading a free-clinic ad that was posted above the handrails. When looking in that direction threatened to make eye contact with Mr. Meat-Underwear, she promptly gazed down at her hands in her lap, framed by the hundreds of black-and-white squares on her sleeves.

She couldn't even check if she was running late. The digital cuff slyly winked "12:00" at her, threatening to expose her sartorial inadequacies to everyone around her in the Metro Levtran car. The cuff clock could have been easily shut off if the sleeve's keyboard would do more than "bloop" pathetically when she punched the underpowered keys. Rolling up the cuff was the only solution.

Not that anyone inside the passenger car was likely to notice her blinking cuff. They all had their noses in newspapers and books. It was pleasantly nostalgic to hear the rustle of newspapers again. You would have thought it was the end of the world when the Chinese and Australians stopped exporting rare-earth metals, halting production of porta-screens. Most people were upset when the little screens started disappearing as malfunctions and fumbling fingers took their toll. Newspapers and books, which had never been fully replaced, had rebounded to fill the void, and Amy liked it. The sound of paper and the smell of books reminded her of her parents reading in the evening at home. When she got her blouse recharged, she'd have to enter a reminder note to get those old DVDs of her mom and dad transferred to Archive format before they became unwatchable. It would be a shame to lose those images from before the Great Pandemic and her parents' passing.

Amy's reverie was interrupted by the automated voice seductively announcing "Robert Street Station." It sounded like they were using Marilyn Monroe's voice this week. She hoped they would pick Cary Grant again soon. His clipped, wry accent always started her day with a smile.

The Levtran's magnetic drive eased to a stop so smoothly that the standing passengers didn't even have to grab the handrails. She remembered, in her youth, riding the buses and watching people "aisle surfing," as her dad called it, trying to stay on their feet as the big white vehicles lurched between stops. Her dad always contended that considering the way the buses jerked, they must have been controlled by "start" and "stop" buttons, instead of accelerator and brake pedals.

As the Levtran magnets powered down, lowering the passenger car to the platform level, the teenager in front of Amy shuffled his meaty unmentionables elsewhere. Amy stood and joined the jostling passengers, who were all trying to get somewhere without being late.

Amy assumed she was late, too, and hurried out into the crisp fall morning. The air seemed to crackle like the leaves skittering along the street before her in the light breeze. The low angle of the morning sunlight and its stark clarity made the leaves of the Best Future Building blaze with colors framed by black shadow. The greens, yellows, oranges, and reds seemed too saturated to be real. It was like one of those old TV advertisements come to life. While she appreciated the ornate 19th century grandeur of buildings like the Union Depot and the clean, Spartan lines of the Town Square Building's 20th century architecture, Amy preferred the Green style of the Best Future Building. It's vine-covered walls and rooftop overspread with grasses and crowned with a small woodlot of aspens had the comfort of an old English cottage combined with the promise of a greenhouse.

If she landed a job there, she could leave behind the limits of the Department of Transportation and the political winds that changed its course every two years. Instead, she'd be able to pursue her career in a stable nonprofit corporate environment of the type that had been pioneered by Minnesota Public Radio back in the 1900s. Using for-profit side businesses, scores of nonprofit corporations had slowly built up endowment funds that allowed them to operate free from the strictures of politics, business, and the public opinion of the moment. These well-intentioned nonprofits even gained enough power to deflect the attempts by business lobbies to strip them of the benefits of being immortal corporate entities like their business counterparts.

These mighty nonprofits had even begun to undo much of the damage created by the global manipulations of the business corporations. The social, public health, economic, and environmental arenas were all starting to show signs of healing.

Of course, there had been Tea Party and Coffee Party protests against "Big Nonprofit." Those loud theaters of the absurd had made their claims that only businesses knew how to give Phil the programmer a good job opportunity, but after the cater-wauling finally died down, the nonprofits were still standing and were still doing their noble work.

While most common people had an underlying fear of big anything, the nonprofits had consistently worked to improve the lives of the working Jills and Jacks. Unlike the elected representatives, the nonprofits had provided leadership on healthy lifestyles, green design for cities, and welfare assistance for the orphans and homeless people. It was these nonprofits, not businesses, that had disinfected the urban centers after the pandemic, allowing the cities to be reborn. Seizing the opportunity, the nonprofits also took steps to reshape these toddling cities so that they featured green spaces for recreation, buildings with tiny carbon footprints, nearby jobs when possible, and the beginning of affordable and sustainable transportation systems. Amy's work in government had helped with those systems when the politics permitted.

If Amy could get a job with the Best Future Foundation, she could pursue projects with 25-year goals to further improve the world for her grandchildren (presuming she eventually met Mr. Right-Enough and started a family, . . . which was never going to happen if she kept going out dressed in the colors of a nuclear warning symbol).

She entered the lobby of the building, and it smelled of the geraniums that hung on hooks around the round, high-ceiling room. The second-story level was a ring of arched windows that allowed in warming sunrays as the days got cooler. When the summer sun returned, the reflective angles built into the glass panes would reflect a large percentage of the sunlight and heat while still allowing this room to be illuminated in a soft glow. The plants would provide cooling with their respiration to supplement the cool air drawn by convection from below-ground chambers as the warm air rose to vents at the top of the dome. Designers in the 18th century had used a similar convection cooling method in the White House, and it had been rediscovered and embraced by the Green Style architects.

Crossing the great hall at the brisk pace of a job candidate who might be late for an interview, Amy passed a handicap elevator on her way to the stairs. There were three giggling schoolgirls inside the small elevator car. Each of them was calling out different floor numbers. The panel lit up indicators for all the floors except one. One of the girls quickly shrieked that number, and the group was engulfed in another giggle fit. With stops scheduled at every floor, the door closed, and the elevator joyride began. Amy remembered doing the same thing during a school field trip when she was 11, not that many years ago, really. That ride had ended with a security guard admonishing them to stop their unhealthy behavior and to take the stairs, so they would grow up lean and strong. It turned out that he was right, and she was lean and strong. Amy climbed the three flights of stairs to the Sustainable Transportation Office without breaking a sweat. Her current office was five flights up, so she was in good shape for one aspect of this job at least.

Pushing open the New Nouveau door of frosted glass and polished metal, Amy found herself in a small anteroom with a desk occupied by an Office Logistics Director about 20 years her senior.  Knowing that this woman's word could easily be the deciding voice on an employment decision, Amy offered her friendliest smile and her hand.

"Hello, I'm Amy Sutton. I'm here for an interview with Drew Schilling. I hope I'm not late," she said in the sweetest tone of voice she could muster.

After the briefest glance at the schedule on her old-fashion desk blotter, the older woman returned a business smile and handshake.

"You're a few minutes early, Ms. Sutton. If you'll have a seat, I'll let Mr. Schilling know you are here," the woman said with well-practiced business decorum.

Amy thanked the woman and made her way to a small cluster of comfortable chairs across the room. She sat down, being sure to stay a bit forward to keep an on-your-toes posture that might be reported to the boss later.

Looking around the room, she made note of a number of photos presented in the quaint flat style to complement the New Nouveau style of the room. There were ribbon cutting ceremonies at Levtran stations. There were photos with teams of scientists in clean suits in front of prototype vehicles. And there was even a woodcut image of an 19th century high-wheel bicycle, befitting the nostalgic look of the room. While the furniture had the look of vintage oak, closer inspection revealed it to be very good bamboo reproductions. They gave the room a warm and homey feel.

Glancing down to smooth her skirt, Amy saw her bare knees, which was to be expected, except when there should have been a yellow skirt covering them. George W. on a hoverski! Her skirt had decided to defect to the land of unpowered clothing along with her blouses. She had intended to change the default setting on the skirt to checkerboard as well, but it was all too obvious that wasn't the only thing she'd forgotten on her to-do list.

She quickly turned her briefcase into a brief cover. Wearing her best outfit, including her good frilly panties, normally added to her confidence in job interviews, but the under things weren't meant for public presentation. How could she escape without creating a picture that would be recounted with guffaws at the coffee machine for years to come? Not to mention that she would be fleeing a job opportunity she had coveted for two years.

Amy decided the only way out was to fake an emergency audio call on her dead sleeve. Then she could make a hasty exit, keeping her briefcase in front of her and the wall close behind her. If only she'd brought along a coat. But with her luck today, it would have burst into flames.

The plan would only get her out of this office. There were still the stairs to descend and a half dozen blocks to walk to the

Levtran station, all on full public display. How was Amy ever going to set foot on the Levtran again after the ride home she would soon be taking? She'd probably have to stand the whole way, too.

Just as Amy started to lift her hand to receive the fake audio call, the office director rose from her chair and walked directly toward Amy. Could this possibly get any worse? How was this woman not going to notice that Amy was now wearing a transparent skirt? While her underwear was trendy and cute, it lacked a lot in business propriety. How was this not going to be mentioned to her no-longer-prospective boss?

The older woman stopped in front of her. Amy stared down at the woman's sensible brown shoes and wished she had selected that big, clunky briefcase with the widescreen monitor rather than the sleek little feminine model that was now failing miserably to hide her assets. A hand, wrinkled from years of life lessons, was lifted in front of her, and in its palm rested a gel-pill power pack.

Amy looked up and saw a knowing smile resting on the woman's lips.

"It's been happening to women since they invented these cursed things. I always keep a couple extra batteries with me," Amy's rescuer said sympathetically.

Amy gratefully accepted this tiny face-saving device, and she quickly opened the waistband pocket to repower her skirt. The office director turned discreetly away while Amy's fingers flew through their vital task. Her skirt flickered and then displayed a cheery yellow once again.

"Who but a lonely lab geek would design the default on clothing to be transparent?" the saint-like woman asked. "I had a dress blink out in a crowded elevator of Hungarian diplomats once, and they were anything but diplomatic about my situation. But they did buy me a very nice dinner that evening."

"How can I ever thank you enough?" Amy gushed.

A melodious ping from the desk interrupted her, and it was followed by a muffled voice that Amy couldn't make out.

"Mr. Schilling will see you now, Ms. Sutton," said the woman, returning to her air of all-business. "But only as much as you intended," she added with wink.

Amy almost regained her composure before she entered the inner office. Her cheeks were still delightfully flushed when she stepped before Drew Schilling. He was seated at his desk facing her. The man was younger than she expected, closer to her age. He had a stylish mid-length haircut and was wearing a suit of cobalt blue, like the color of Como Lake on a blue-sky summer day. The mellow baritone of his voice saying, "Please have a seat," caused a surprising flutter somewhere inside her chest. But he did not rise to shake her hand as was customary, giving birth to a small doubt about the outcome of this interview. Pushing that twinge aside, she focused on presenting herself as she'd been practicing to do for the last two evenings.

The interview began with the usual short question-and-answer period, confirming the details of her résumé. When the inevitable "Tell me about yourself," request finally arrived,

Amy launched into a first-rate recounting of her undergraduate education in urban planning at Macalester. She recounted the student project to turn a shutdown brothel into a cultural center, which had been half-way successful. She regaled him with a list of graduate courses and seminars she'd attended at the Dayton School for Societal Improvement. Amy even offered him a copy of her thesis on providing accessible transportation to combat poverty and urban decay, which he politely declined. That was to be expected. Who reads a thesis after it's finished? Keeping up her forward momentum, Amy boldly narrated a 3D movie from her briefcase, detailing the successful projects she'd helmed at the Department of Transportation, including the development of the bicycle highway. She showed how that six-mile route was now hosting 30,000 bicycle commuters each day, cutting the use of gasoline by an estimated 10,000 gallons daily, more than 3.5 million gallons a year. That put $21 million back in the pockets of those commuters, about $700 per person. Amy was certain that her interviewer would be impressed to see that she had made a real-world difference in the lives of 30,000 lives, a contribution that would continue to grow in years ahead.

But the opposite seemed to be true. Amy was disappointed to see Drew Schilling glance away a couple times during her carefully rehearsed accounting of herself, and he seemed decidedly distracted. She wasn't holding his attention, a very bad sign when one was a job seeker. She turned up her peppiness a notch as she finished with an irrefutable argument for why she was the best possible candidate for the job opening.

After she had finished flashing her life history before his eyes, the man who was unlikely to be her future boss asked a couple questions about people she knew in professional organizations and if she had studied with a few college professors he had met. He did not seem to be listening to any of the answers. Amy knew she had failed to impress, but kept up her best game face as the interview wobbled to a halt.

"Well, Ms. Sutton, despite your excellent qualifications and body of work, I don't have a position for you in my division," Drew Schilling said with a disappointed tone.

This was the perfect flaming-crash ending to a train wreck of a morning, thought Amy as she reinforced her crumbling game face.

"But I believe that you are the prefect person to head up our new ultralight car project. The job is yours if you want it. If you do, I'll arrange for you to meet with Jen Horton, our president. It's really just a formality; the decision is mine to make," he assured her, "and, of course, yours."

Amy's on-your-toes posture served her well as she leapt out of her chair.

"Oh, yes. I'm very interested . . . I mean, I'll take the job," she said with the words tumbling out.

She thrust her hand across the desk, but immediately feared she'd fallen on her face just before the finish line. Drew Schilling didn't rise to extend his hand as she'd anticipated. Finding herself leaning over the wide desk with an unwelcomed hand outstretched, Amy awkwardly withdrew it, unsure of what to say or do.

The man on the other side of the desk looked troubled and didn't meet her gaze. Back to flaming disaster, bodies strewn everywhere, and fathers and mothers weeping. Why hadn't she just stayed in her seat and thanked him? Somehow she had managed to snatch defeat from the jaws of victory.

"I am . . . ah, . . . I mean . . . " Amy stammered incoherently, stepping backwards toward her seat. Maybe there would be a trap door, and she could conveniently fall from the face of the planet, never to be seen again.

"Ms. Sutton, I'm in a very uncomfortable situation here."

Had she blundered through some unspoken social barrier? Had she invaded his bubble of personal comfort? Was he one of the hyper-phobics who saw ever person as a potential pandemic-disease vector? Or was he just repulsed by her personally? Did it really matter if it was any or all of these reasons or something else entirely? Her eleventh-hour failure was the clear result in any event.

The back of her calves found the chair she'd been sitting in, and she stopped, wondering what she should do next. Retreat. When facing certain defeat, retreat as soon as possible. She reached for her briefcase as she propped up a smile on her face and spoke.

"Well, thank you for your time, Mr. Schilling. I think I should be . . . " she managed to say with a reasonable amount of steadiness before she was interrupted.

"This isn't the way I usually welcome a new employee," he said, finally looking her in the eyes again.

New employee?! Not shame-filled rejection? Not ego-crushing failure? Not a psyche-scarring catastrophe?

Drew Schilling rose to his feet and extending a congratulatory hand in his stylish haircut, cobalt-blue suit, and . . . red-polka-dot pants. Amy stifled a laugh, and clasped his hand without glancing down at his pants . . . well, maybe just once or twice.

Embarrassed, Drew shook his head as he looked down at his buffoonish attire.

"I've been so busy lately, I forgot to put my slacks on the charger. I set them to this default, so I'd notice when they needed charging. I noticed right after I told Marjorie to send you in," he explained.

Amy covered her mouth with her hand to hide an unseemly grin, but her dancing eyes betrayed all.

"Do you think, as your first official duty, you could bring me one of those power packs Marjorie keeps in her desk," he asked.

"Of course, Mr. Schilling. Will there be anything else?" she said, with only a hint of impishness.

"Keep this story away from the coffee machine, and we're going to be good friends," he offered. "I might even buy you lunch." There was a pleading look in the back of his comfortable brown eyes.

"Yes, sir," said Amy as she spun on her heel and headed for the outer office of her new boss. On the way home, maybe she would treat herself to a new blouse and suit . . . with some extra power packs.

# The Fall of the World's Own Optimist

By Bob Lipski

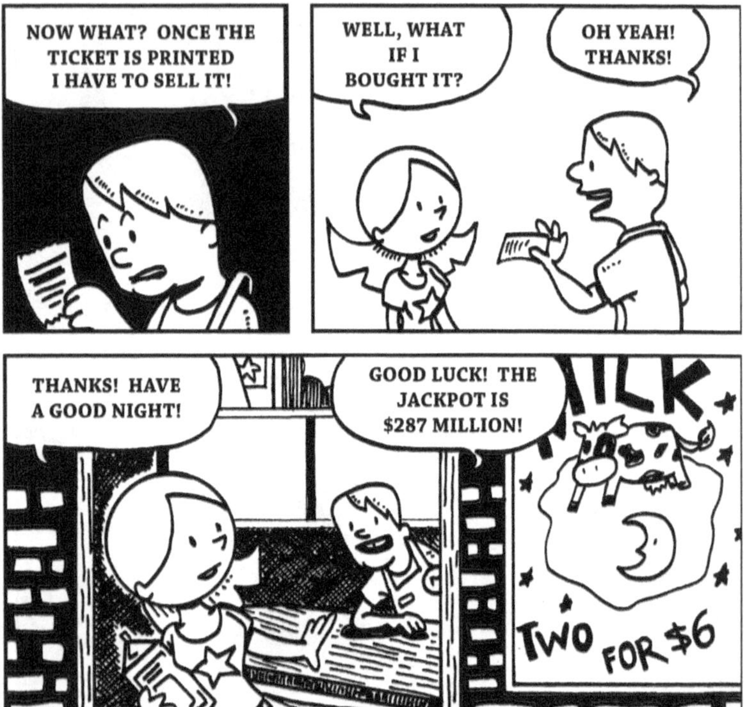

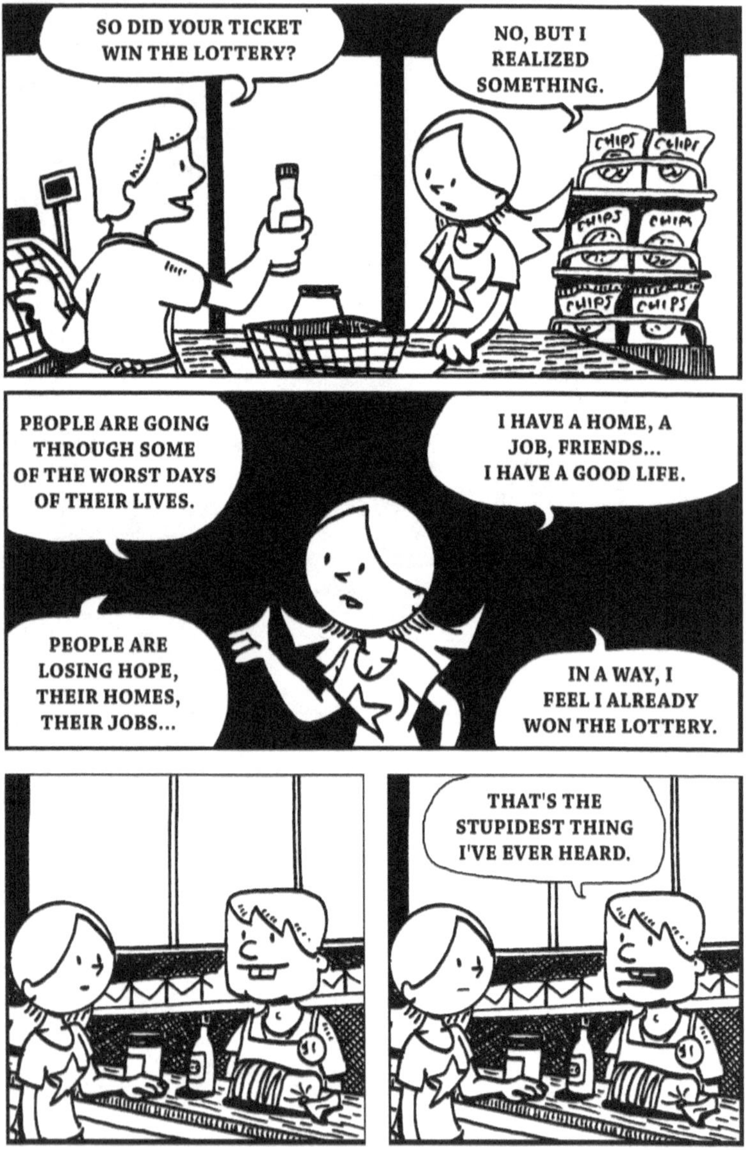

# Bullseye, Inc
By Brian D. Garrity

Zelda realized she was late for work again, beneath a frigid morning sky, where low, thick clouds blazed with a patchwork of roving advertisements. Corporations reveled in these gloomy stretches of weather, aggressively competing for available promotional cloudspace. The recognition software guiding the laser painters was able to match the shapes of their respective products or logos to the billowing ephemera. Unfortunately, competition between products for similarly-shaped ad space often resulted in a seizure-inducing chromatic lightning battle, like the one now, crackling in the air between Coke and Pepsi.

Zelda averted her gaze from the stuttering anomaly and scanned the shifting view out the train window for the brand of her new employer. There, prominently above all others, reigned the familiar Bullseye logo—a blue ring encircling a solid red disk pierced by blue arrow.

Sighing, she scanned the fellow commuters surrounding her on the overcrowded light-rail car, a khaki-pantsed, Bullseye-Blue-shirted legion and endured the mixture of hostile and malevolent glimpses her presence garnered.

It wasn't that she was inappropriately dressed, nor was she in any way un-presentable. With soft sculpted cheekbones, large hazel eyes, full sensual lips, and long, smooth Modigliani neck, she could have been a model for some media ideal of physique. What attracted the ire of these strangers was her platinum hair and porcelain skin-tone.

As one of the last Caucasians, Zelda was an aberration.

Over the last few hundred years, mixing of the races had yielded a planet-wide, beige populous. *The mocha race,* as her friend Hondo, a typical statistical representative, jokingly called it. At least they shared a sense of humor about her skin tone. That, and a covert past from the previous revolution.

She mused that, ironically, it was a collective memory of racism that helped bond contemporary society. Prejudice, after all, was still prejudice, something she'd dealt with her entire life. Yet Caucasian intolerance still permeated pop culture, the ubiquitous corporate media and hip-hop music industry promoting a past, to Zelda, that never was.

The collapsing facades of a strip-mall zipped by, and she recalled the archaic private businesses that had thrived there during her childhood before the Big Collapse and subsequent

Global Corporatism. *Before we sold out our freedom for stabilization,* she thought, glancing in despair at her own matching uniform.

Attempting to disregard the surrounding acidic glares, she sighed again thinking; *This world is no longer mine.*

*They come to get the things. They need the things. The things are made a long way away, and they come in boxes. Some big, real big, and lots small, and the men in the trucks bring the boxes. The men bring the boxes in the store, and they open them and put the things on the shelves, but it's not my job to help, because I'm special. My job is special.*

*Isaac and Deckard are special too, like me, but they have chairs with wheels that drive them around, and I like them a lot. Isaac is my boss. Isaac's boss is Ryan, and I like him too, but he's not special, like us. Ryan gave me the nice blue shirt to wear with the circles and the arrow, and the pants that are brown, and the soft shoes with all the little holes in them so my feet don't sweat and smell bad.*

*Ryan gave me the stick with the ball on the end that is my job, and I use the ball to rub out the marks on the floor that the other people's shoes make, so the store can look clean and nice, and I smile and say hi to all the people, especially the pretty girls. I like the pretty girls, like Candy and Monique, who work with me, but I don't like the white girl, Zelda.*

*Lots of people come to the store, and I am always working with the ball to make the floor clean, and I smile and say hi to all the people and the pretty girls. They come to get the things…*

Ryan's belt-com squelched an angry tone followed by a sputtering voice, "Can we get another checkout on level two? Please!" He cast an annoyed glance about and spotted two uniformed workers in the midst of banal gossip, and marched up close, deliberately violating personal space. "Monique, is your com on?"

She stared back in incomprehension.

Pointing vaguely towards the up escalator, Ryan padded his voice with deliberate calm. "I need you on checkout lane twenty-two, OK?" She nodded blankly and moved off, his voice following. "More smiles in the aisles, Monique."

*God, these people are just fucking zombies.* He snorted, a gesture he was unaware of, but one that was noted and mimicked by numerous co-workers. *If they only knew, could only comprehend what it takes to make this place run. This, the flagship for the largest corporate conglomerate on earth. If only they realized the burden of responsibility I shoulder trying to make the cogs of this great machinery turn smoothly.*

He watched the hunched figure of the little mongoloid guy, Nathan, scuttle between throngs of browsing patrons, stabbing the scuff-marks off the floor with a broom-handle, and slit tennis ball on the end.

*If only they could all be more like Nathan, more like those other cripps, Deckard and Isaac. No other distractions in their lives just total dedication to the corporation.* This reminded him of something, and he consulted his watch, snorting. *Not like that white-witch Zelda, late again!* He inwardly cursed the equal employment policy of the company and walked up to Nathan and gave him a hearty slap on the back.

"Great job, Nathan. Keep it up!"

Nathan looked up, smiled through the warped panes of his face, drooled, and farted loudly.

The view from the eighty-sixth floor penthouse of the Vikings Tower over the sprawl of what was once referred to as the Twin Cities was magnificent. Digby Gentlebottom III uncharacteristically recognized the light-sculpted vista beyond his windows as something to take note of.

*Huge things were afoot.*

Feeling the rush of the impending acquisition, he noted approvingly the progress the rebuilding projects had achieved in stitching together the physical damage inflicted on the city by the last revolution. The infidel revolt had been crushed, and the rise of New Morality pulled together a society on the verge of collapse. Sure, a few heads had rolled, but that was the cost of civilization. The world was healing. The corporation in no small part responsible. That and the new fundamentalist administration led by President King.

A familiar tone chimed from his deskpad indicating the

arrival of a class-one conference call. Digby Gentlebottom III, CEO of Bullseye Inc., straightened the tie on a suit that cost over three times the annual income of most of his employees and framed himself strategically before the window's panoramic spectacle.

*This was the backstage to history. The world changes today.*

He took the call.

The store was testament to the evolution of human distraction. At least to Zelda's eyes and ears.

Occupying two square city blocks and seven full stories, the place was practically a city unto itself—every square inch awash in the relentless glare of daylight-balanced fluorescent grids illuminating aggressively colored product labels, each meant to wrest attention from its competitor and stacked in dizzying patterns along countless tiered shelves. Kinetic displays disgorged sound and movement into the milling horde of customers and the nearly equal number of employees that darted around them, belt-com's bursting with static and garbled commands.

Hurrying past the in-store clinic, the portrait studio, and the movie theater, Zelda pinched at the bridge of her nose, already feeling the onset of a headache. A high-tech wheelchair zipping between bodies, its occupant a spidery tangle of atrophied limbs, halted inches from her feet.

Isaac sneered up at her through archaic glasses, magnifying the contempt shining behind his eyes.

"This is not showing proper team spirit, Zelda. You're

twenty minutes late."

"I know, Isaac. I'm sorry but the light-rail was delayed…"

"Deckard had to cover for you, and he missed his break. Go relieve him now."

"That's where I was…"

The chair whipped a silent half-circle and slipped back through the crowd.

Beside her, the card rack waxed into one of its eerie synchronicities. Thousands of banal greeting tunes trapped in the pages played simultaneously, a cacophony that drove a shearing spike of pain behind her eyes.

Zelda shifted through the walkers, the rollers, waddlers, and shufflers, the majority rendered zombie-like by sheer presence of the products, or distracted by thumb-jockeying screens of various handheld devices. She pressed her way toward the music section, passing a huddle of Bullseye-blue shirted co-workers being addressed by a superior, dressed in civvies, tone patiently condescending. It was a familiar technique to publicly browbeat lower echelons under the auspices of updating managerial directive. She forged on, passing Nathan vigorously rubbing out a scuffmark.

Enclosed by his own even higher-tech version of Isaac's wheels, Deckard waited, grinning slyly, quilling the peak of a faux-hawk with his one good hand. Zelda braced herself and stepped up.

"I know I'm late Deckard. I'm sorry. You can take a break now."

The chair swiveled. "Twenty-three minutes, Zelda. That's a demerit."

"What?"

Ryan materialized behind Deckard laying a hand on the backrest. "That's right, Zelda, Deckard has been promoted to music manager. He's your new boss."

Hissing to herself, counting to five, she breathed in slowly and smiled. "That's great, sir. Congratulations."

Ryan snorted.

Deckard flinched, jerked his ambulatory hand. "One more demerit left, Zelda. Use it wisely." The chair slid away.

Ryan turned waving dismissively. "Get to work, team member." Waiting until she started away, he said, "Zelda?"

Stopping. "Sir?"

"Important team meeting today in the auditorium. Level ten. Odd members at ten-thirty, even at eleven hundred. You are?"

She sighed. "Odd."

He smiled. "Right."

*About the floor job, it never gets done. This is good. The store tells me where Eugene left off before me, and I start there, and when I come back to where I started, the floor needs to be cleaned again. It's like the things on the shelves. It's like everything here. A cycle, a circle, like this planet. Nothing ever starts or stops or changes. I like it a lot like that. It makes me feel needed because I am a part of everything that has to get done here. Here, I am important.*

    *Very important.*

"Miss Tessmacher, would you join me please?"

Digby Gentlebottom III toyed with the Real-D display on his desk as the door to his suite dissolved with a musical flourish, and his personal assistant, Lyra Tessmacher slipped expertly into the space before him. A sublime combination of efficiency and sexuality, she represented the pinnacle of her trade. Elegantly dropping into the facing chair, quickly arranging several electronic tablets on her lap, she wet her lips with a very long tongue.

"And how did the meeting go?"

He poked a finger through a revolving image of the moon. "Well. It went ...well."

She inhaled. "What did you lose?"

"Controlling interest." He turned off the display. "Not important, though. We're all one big happy family now."

Leaning over the desk, she displayed symmetrically calculated cleavage. "And did you finally get to meet the CEO of Terran Media Control?"

He shook his head, "Christ, those people at TMC are cloak and dagger. They even had the visuals encrypted. Only way I could confirm their identity was through the security procedures we'd agreed."

"Doesn't that seem strange?"

Digby shrugged, "An empire vast as that can pretty much operate anyway they want. We do. Doesn't matter. We've finally eliminated archaic, inefficient capitalism." He straightened in the chair. "Not like there's been any real corporate competition in decades. Only difference between Coke and Pepsi is the design on the label, but people need the illusion of choice."

Miss Tessmacher leaned back, re-crossing toned legs beneath her sheer skirt.

"They just can't be trusted to make that choice."

"Right!" He slapped the desk's surface, pushed the over-stuffed leather chair back, eyes blazing. "And now Bullseye Incorporated owns the entire planet!" He smiled professionally. "Plus, I got us something else in the deal. Something... wonderful."

"Tell," she tensed.

"I want a major press conference on the roof tomorrow evening. All the networks. All *our* networks. Handle the arrangements." Squirming, he worked the buttons of his blazer. "Miss Tessmacher, I am dealing with some seriously petrified wood here. Would you be so kind as to see me through a happy ending before I impart you with that exclusive knowledge?"

"Of course." Setting aside the tools of her trade, she stood, slinked around his desk and sank slowly to her knees.


Behind the podium, Ryan looked out at the upturned faces in a sea of Bullseye-Blue, spotted Zelda's conspicuous pallor, an aberrant pixel on the display of humanity before him, and snorted, the noise booming back through the sound system.

He noted the reaction.

"Team members, today is a truly special day. I come to you with amazing news. This morning, Bullseye Incorporated announced news of a merger with Terran Media Control, the largest ever, one that is guaranteed to endow us all with generous future prosperity. To commemorate this monumental event, a celebratory reception will be held on the roof of the Viking's Tower tomorrow night, attended by celebrities and corporate moguls from extended points of the globe." He stepped back indicating the LDT wall behind him that washed to life with color and sound.

Gentlebottom's office was a fashion spread. The view beyond had been expansively augmented. Digby himself appeared model-esque, sculpted in light and towering over the gathering.

"There are events throughout history that punctuate periods of great change, and I ask you to mark today's date as one. Citizens, fellow employees, for the first time in human history, the planet is united. Our recent amalgamation with TMC marks a new era of stability, and as parent company to the new world, we wish to share our jubilation. Tomorrow night, at Bullseye's world headquarters, a celebration like no other will be held, a full media event brought to you live with special appearances by President King, and Archbishop Lombardy from the National Church of Athletics."

Digby Gentlebottom III's face swooped in to cover the entire wall, and he winked slyly. "Capping the occasion will be a special surprise, one that must be beheld to be believed. At precisely nine o'clock, I invite *all* residing in the North American continent to look for the moon." He smiled, his perfect row of teeth like monoliths over the room, fading as Ryan stepped back into the spotlight, voice choked with amplified emotion.

"As manager of our flagship store here in Central City, I have been extended the honor to attend the gala tomorrow, proudly representing you."

Backing off the stage, he noted the triumvirate of Isaac and Deckard flanking Nathan, dead center of the gathering, an utterly alien expression of comprehension on the Mongol's face.

*The things are almost ready. The things we have waited so long for. The last things. To make it all together.*

*It is almost time.*

*To reveal.*

*Metamorphosis.*

"Those pigfuckers!"

Hondo ducked the shoe Zelda kicked across her tiny room, and again as it ricocheted back by his face, springing the short nappy dreads covering his head.

"Zeld's…"

She caught herself reflected in the wall mirror, still in her work-shirt, and tore it off in disgust, standing before him in a black bra. "You know what it is, don't you? It's Tyranny."

Cautiously reseating himself on one of the two chairs in the single-room structure, Hondo frowned, scratching at graying muttonchops. "Actually, think it's closer to a Corporate Monarchy."

"You know what I mean, Hon." Throwing arms out to her sides, she brought exquisite life to the undergarment. "It's indentured slavery! They got us all living like drone bees, in these…these tubes!"

He shrugged. "Got an apartment like everyone else."

"*Com*-partment! It's a fucking *com*-partment! An apartment is what *you and I* grew up in! *Ahhh*!" Zelda noticed the khaki's, jerked them off, and kicked them again by his head. Now only clad in bra and pink thong, she dropped onto the edge of her foldout wall-bed.

"What happened to the revolution, Hon? What happened to individuality? What happened to the band?"

He swallowed and licked his lips. "You were there, Zelda. We lost."

She rose, walked to where he was sitting and touched his shoulders. "We lost a lot of good people."

"Alright. Hold up, yo?" Hondo sighed, running eyes up her body. "What you doing here Zeld's? The striptease? May not register on your screen, but you *know* I'm of the male species, and I believe you also know how I feel about wanting to take your creamy thighs…"

"Got it!" She backed off picking up a discarded slipover dress from the floor. His eyes followed. "Sorry Hon. Just upset. Pissed off." The garment was applied to her physique. "I miss 'em, you know? I miss Barris. I miss Ray and the Goose. I miss my sister."

He flinched, attention suddenly on a finger picking at his

shoe. "Um, well…yeah, me too. I think…I think about Sliver every day, and how she, you know…"

"I know." Sitting again, she chuckled sadly. "Hate to say, but I really miss Dante, too, the twisted genius." Tapping herself on the chest twice, she spread a palm. "Heart, soul, and brain, he almost took it around the corner."

Hondo's Cee-Phone played a strangely familiar riff.

"Damn, the man's good." Hitting a key, Hondo rose and moved to the entry as it chimed. "Thought the shit goin' down tonight might get you a little bristled. Invited a friend to add a little cheer."

Disengaging security, he opened the door to reveal a warped, diminutive form occupying the frame. "Haven't lost the flair for the dramatic, I see."

"Ah…well yes…timing is of the essence."

Zelda shrieked. "Dante?"

The small man hobbled in on a gimp leg, greasy hair slicked back over a rat-like skull, thick eyeglasses sliding down the bridge of his nose. "It is wonderful to see you again, Zelda."

Hondo closed the door, "Enter, public enemy number one."

Staring, Zelda shook her head, "I thought you were dead."

"Call me Lazarus," he pushed glasses back up.

Rushing in, she crumpled him to her breast. "God! How did you stay hidden for so long?"

"Uhm…well…" Muffled by her cleavage, "…friends in low places."

Hondo chuckled moving past.

Straight-arming him, she nodded, "It's the merger, right?"

"We need to access the roof. It's almost nine-o'clock. We have to see."

Hondo cracked knuckles, "Why's that, Dante?"

Settling frames back into place, he swept them with a magnified gaze, "Gentlebottom specified to look for the moon. Tonight is the new moon."

He blinked.

"It should be completely invisible."

The crown of the Viking's Tower was enveloped by a swarm of luminous hovering vehicles, battering the air in anxious waves through an encroaching twilight, capturing content for the media, transporting VIPs to and from the reception.

Wandering the rooftop, witnessing the spectacle, Ryan tried to contain the infectious rapture practically oozing from the surrounding glitterati as he worked the meet-and-greets, pressing flesh, the smile on his face actually beginning to cramp from overuse.

The evening had proceeded perfectly. Beginning with Gentlebottom's introduction, basically a recap of last night's 'cast; followed by another teaser regarding the gala's climax; and finishing with a jaw-dropping production by the corporation's newest music unveiling, Diced Cube, a Hip-Hop trio. President King delivered an ebullient endorsement of the occasion, effectively smoke-screening the fact that he was now rendered a mere puppet, and Archbishop Lombardy imparted a moving prayer to mark the event, covertly consigning support for the Vikings in the upcoming game.

Now the fireworks. Ryan walked both above and beneath an atmosphere alive with light and sound.

"It's time," Miss Tessmacher strode briskly up to Digby Gentlebottom III's side and handed him a paper-thin Titanium App-Pad. "Cloud-scrubbers have completed their run. They guarantee at least two hours of clear sky."

He nodded, "And the projection crew?"

"On standby." She picked a stray hair from a perfect lapel, "Waiting on your password."

"Excellent," Making his way slowly back to the stage, Digby noted the cameras turn toward him, lights following, crowd suddenly hushed in anticipation. He toed the edge, facing his audience, thrust his hands into his pockets in a deliberately casual gesture, and flashed them his trillion-dollar smile.

"And now, the *pièce de résistance*—a small demonstration of what a unified world can achieve." Thumbing the App-Pad's screen, he waved it behind him.

The blazing cityscape suddenly and silently dimmed, exposing for the first time since the metropolis had emerged the fine quilting of stars against the Milky Way above. An appreciative sigh escaped the collective.

"To say that we make history today would be a gross

understatement. The *history* of mankind has been plagued with conflict and violence since it has gone on record, a plague that has run unchecked for millennia. Now…finally…we are at peace."

Pausing dramatically, Digby Gentlebottom III thumbed a new sequence and swept his arms up to the heavens. "People of the earth, workers of Bullseye Incorporated, tonight not only do we own the world…we own the moon!"

An absence against the firmament that was the shadow of the moon slowly crawled with light, running a spectrum of color across its chasms and craters, coalescing with a dazzling flare into the concentric circles of the Bullseye logo.

The crowd's reaction was immediate and great, and from the metropolis and the world beyond, came a rising roar of awe.

Digby bent out of mike-shot into Tessmacher's ear, "Where the fuck is the arrow?"

Blinking rapidly from the sky to her pad, she said in a small voice, "I don't understand."

An azure flash on the western horizon sizzled into the missing graphic, a Bullseye-Blue spear that arced a slow trajectory towards the center of the moon.

Digby's face lost its composure, "That's not ours."

"It is not. It's *ours*."

He and Tessmacher turned to discover they were sharing the stage with three other figures—two apparent quadriplegics, flanking a man of indeterminate age displaying obvious symptoms of Downs Syndrome.

All were dressed in the uniforms of lowly floor workers.

Ryan's brain was spinning.

First, the muting of the city's lights, then the logo on the moon, the flying arrow, and now, his special employees sharing the stage with Gentlebottom. It was too much.

Overwhelmed, not quite understanding what he was doing, Ryan rushed past the distracted security, up the stage to stand before Isaac, Deckard, and Nathan.

"What the hell are you three doing here?"

The chairs moved protectively forward, Isaac jittering to a stop. "I would watch what you say... *manager*."

"Yeah..." Deckard pointed, "...show a little respect for the new CEO of earth."

"What?" Ryan, Gentlebottom, and Tessmacher said in unison.

"That's right, *Terrans*. Nathan is the Head of Terran Media Control."

"And now... I own controlling interest in Bullseye!" Stepping into a wash of light, Nathan, dressed in logo'd shirt, khaki's, and green plastic shoes, raised the tennis ball-tipped broom-handle.

"People of earth. Fear not. We originate from farther away than you can imagine, but have been with you peacefully for millennia, slowly shaping your leaders, society, and culture away from your primitive destructive individualism, to a model that more conforms to our own—one of longstanding cooperative efficiency—so that we may share with you the rare and valuable resources of this planet. A symbiosis of our two cultures *will* be mutually beneficial. I might remind you here that this is an agreement arrived at through *your* laws and systems. We strongly advise you to honor this contract. It is not our intention for this to be a hostile takeover, and we look forward to your cooperation in the changes we plan to implement."

The arrow crossed the logo's corona as Ryan crumpled Italian silk lapels in his fists. "Gentlebottom, you bastard, you outsourced earth to the aliens!"

A hysterical squall rose from the gathering, the city; they looked up.

The alien arrow scored a bullseye. The moon shuddered, bulged slightly in the middle, and slowly squashed into an ellipsoid.

Nathan lowered his arms, "Uh oh."


"Well, this changes everything."

Dante wiped his glasses on the tail of his shirt, the three of them still on the roof after the broadcast's unprecedented shutdown, watching the debris of the moon spread across the horizon.

"Ya think?"

"So…yeah, Dante?" Hondo glanced at Zelda. "What happens now?"

"Oh…I imagine there will be a sizeable amount of tectonic

activity." He replaced the lenses, which immediately slid down the bridge of his nose. "Tidal activity. Tsunamis, climate changes. Incalculable trickle-down effects."

Zelda whistled, "I'm sensing some anarchy in our future."

"I like," Hondo produced a highly illegal cigarette, savoring the tobacco's smell for a beat before popping it into his mouth, "Stir this shit up."

"In exile, I worked up plans for a very special project," Dante spoke to the spectacle above. "This appears to be a watershed moment to put them into implementation."

Lighting the smoke, the smell stimulating Zelda's memories of clubs' back stages, band practice, old friends, Hondo tucked an arm around her waist. "Zeld's, I've been thinking."

"Did that hurt?"

"Very funny."

"Sorry," She leaned into her friend. "What were you thinking, Hon?"

He blew smoke out into the twilight. "We really should get the band back together."

Beneath them the terra firma lurched lazily with a rolling boom, while above, sunlight from the approaching day caught the farthest edge of Earth's new ring.

# Zombielzebub: Hell's Invasion

By John Beckmann

# Zombielzebub: Hell's Invasion

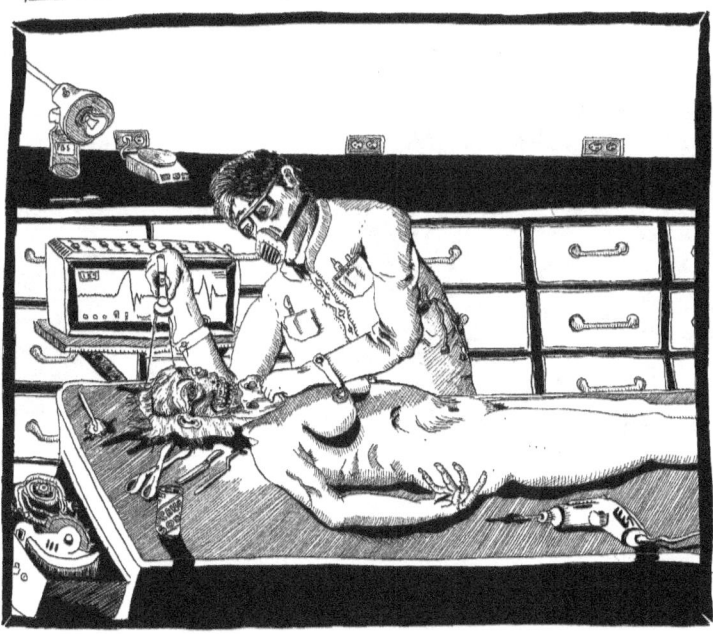

# Zombielzebub: Hell's Invasion

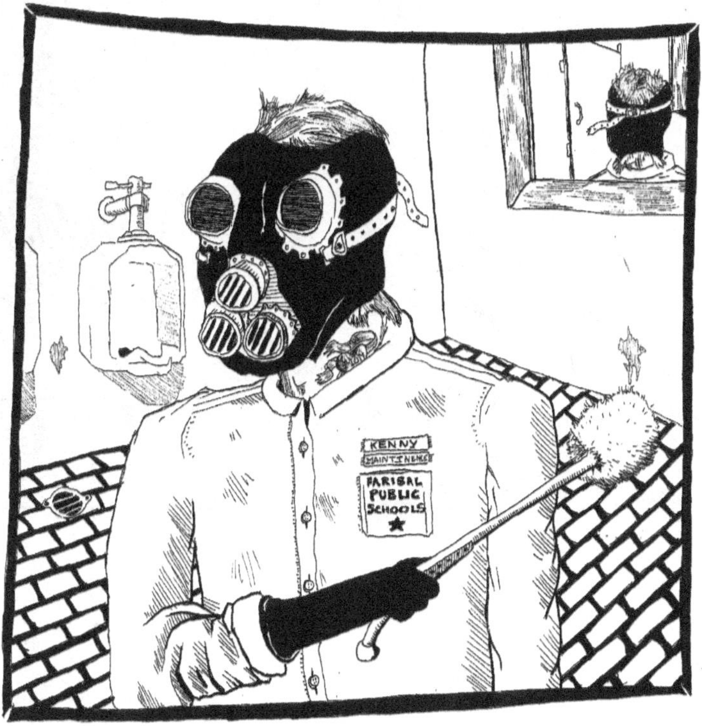

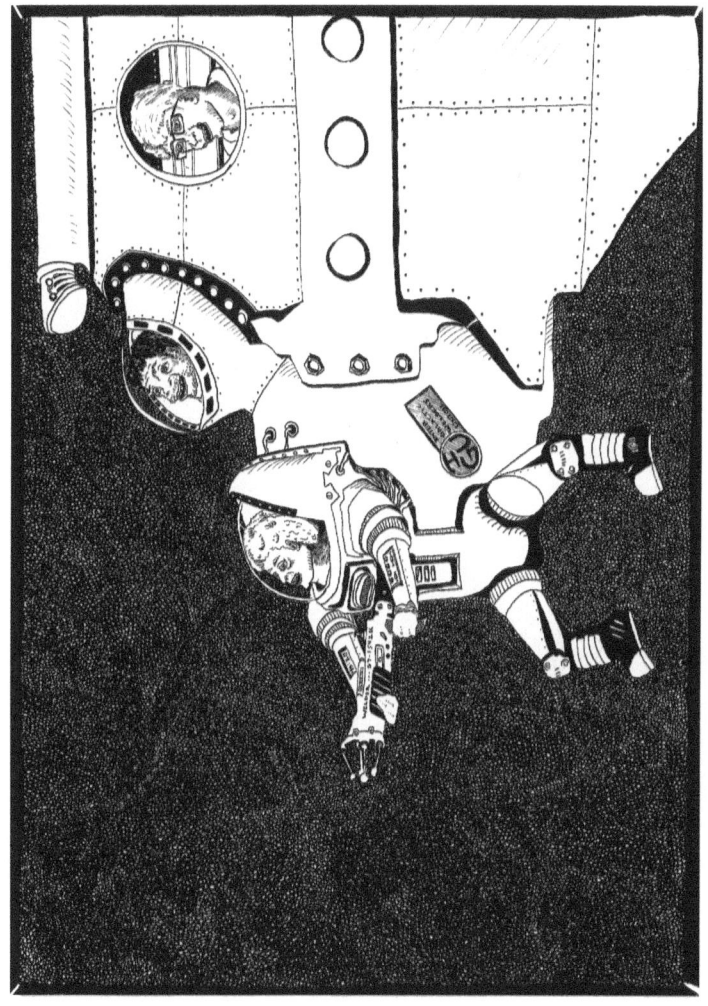

# Little Hawk
By Erica Lindquist
& Aron Christensen

"Why you hurrying home? No one's there for you!"

"Mum's working out late again, yeah? I got something for her to work on in my pants," jeered another one of Sullis' friends. The gap-toothed teen thrust his hips suggestively. "Her work comes cheap, don't it? Could probably keep her busy all night for ten-cen!"

"Fly off!" Logan shouted. He hurled himself at the nearest boy, not one of those who had spoken – not this time, at least – but all of Sullis' gang were the same. Bigger, meaner and stronger than scrawny ten-year-old Logan Centra. He bounced off the much larger older boy and sprawled on the cracked pavement.

Sullis laughed sharply. He was six or so years older than Logan, but at least three times bigger, with broad shoulders and pocked skin. His gang tightened their circle around Logan. Sullis waggled his tongue insolently at the boy on the ground.

"Got something to say to your mum, Logan? Why don't you tell me?" he taunted. "I'll be seeing her later tonight. I'll take real good care of her, don't worry."

Logan's eyes streamed with furious tears. He pulled his feet under him, but another of Sullis' boys – a wiry, ruddy-faced young man – kicked Logan in the chest and sent him tumbling back to the grease-stained roadside. Cars raced and rattled by, their drivers taking no notice of the boys fighting just a few yards away. Logan wheezed and tried to jump at Sullis again. He swung a poorly-aimed punch at the gang's leader. Sullis took a single step back, laughing again.

"You can't fight worth a turd," he said, then leered at Logan. "But then, what else you expect from the son of a whore? I bet you know how to ass about just fine. Gonna be a rental like your mum?"

"She's not a whore!" Logan cried. He cast about for a suitable insult. His heart was racing so fast in his chest that he couldn't hear the individual beats anymore, just a thin hum like the pulse of a bird. "But I bet you are! And your buyers don't even know you're a boy until they've got your pants down!"


Logan could only see through one eye. The other was simply too swollen. He could only open it a crack and even then, everything seemed muddy and red. Still, he knew the route home from school well enough that he could have made it with both eyes shut. Logan really hoped he wouldn't have to test that.

The sun was setting behind the steep mountains that surrounded Highwind like a crown of great stone blades. The stars would come out before long, but it would be some hours more before they would shine with light enough to pierce the thick miasma of smoke and other pollutants that filled the city air.

Highwind looked not unlike a pile of old boxes, discarded but not empty. Like so many Prian cities, most of the houses were cheap, mass produced as flimsy, barely habitable temporary shelters. They were only designed to stand for a year or two before replacement. Most of the thin-walled cubes or squat apartment blocks were fifty years old or more. They had been patched and repaired so many times that the walls seemed quilted in blotchy rust, water-stained aluminum and flaking paint. The roads of Highwind were as cracked and piebald as the houses matched by the cars and pedestrians that traveled them.

Logan tripped a few times on the uneven concrete, once coming dangerously close to stumbling into a chem dealer lounging on the street corner. The woman glared at Logan through lank blonde hair and prodded the boy onward with a boot against his backside. He moved on without looking back.

Logan climbed the creaking stairs that zig-zagged across the face of his building and reached the faded green door of his mother's apartment. For a panicked moment, he couldn't find his keys. *Had they fallen out of his pocket when Sullis kicked him?* No, Logan found them a moment later in his back pocket. The locks took some effort, but he muscled the door open with a grunt.

The small apartment was empty, of course. That much of Sullis' stupid taunting had been true. His mother was working late, as usual. Logan dropped his crack-screened school datadex on the couch and went to the kitchen for some ice. He broke a few cubes from a tray in the freezer and wrapped them in a towel from beside the sink.

Back in the living room, Logan flopped down on the couch. On the other end, his guitar twanged at the jostling as though gently admonishing its young master. The boy considered playing, but his hands ached and his ribs hurt. He closed his eyes, but couldn't sleep. Logan sat up and pulled the guitar into his lap, curling his stiff fingers around the worn wooden neck and began to play.

"My God! What happened?"

Logan looked up with a start. He had lost all track of time. Lynn Centra stood in the doorway with her hands pressed to her mouth and her cheeks bloodlessly pale. A bag of groceries lay forgotten at her feet. Logan sat up, wincing. He touched his face and felt the crumbly crackle of dried blood.

Lynn rushed to her son's side and grabbed the towel from the couch beside him. The cloth was still damp from the long-melted ice. She caught Logan's chin in gentle fingers and turned him to face her. "Oh, sweetheart. What happened?"

"Sullis," he mumbled. His lips felt stiffer and more swollen than before. The ice hadn't done a very good job, Logan decided. "He said things about you…"

"Shhh, it doesn't matter." She wiped lightly at the blood on his split lip. "God, Logan. You shouldn't be fighting. It doesn't matter what the other boys say about me. They're just children."

"But they called you a…" Logan couldn't even bring himself to say the word. It made him so angry just to think it. "It's not true!"

"No, sweetheart, it's not. I know that and so do you. It doesn't matter what anyone else thinks. Don't fight with them, Logan. If the older boys try to corner you, just run. It doesn't do any good to fight." He mumbled a noncommittal reply and didn't meet his mother's eye. She sighed. "Look at all this mess. Why don't you go wash up while I get dinner ready?"

"Okay."

Logan showered and put on cleaner clothes, then came back into the living room. Lynn was in the kitchen, warming a small bowl of noodles and some red sauce. She smiled at the boy and nodded to the cupboard.

"Are you intact enough to set the table?" she asked.

"Sure," Logan answered.

"My brave little hawk." Lynn smiled at her son.

He pulled open the cupboard, the doors wobbling on tarnished, crooked hinges, and stood up on his toes to reach the bowls on the top shelf. Lynn owned only one set of dishes, four glass plates and four bowls with four matching teacups and saucers. They were her pride and joy – after Logan, of course.

Her mother's mother had bought them from a Dailon who claimed they were antiques all the way from Axis. It probably wasn't true, but the glass was beautiful and delicate, finished in a rich blue like the evening sky.

Logan carried the bowls very carefully to the little table under the apartment's single window. Thick bars welded to the frame outside cut the view of the street outside into long slats like a paneled painting in one of the Union chapels. The sky was dark now, black as ink. There was only one moon out tonight, Unos. It hung in the darkness like a lopsided yellow grin, smirking down at the Prians scrabbling in the rocky dirt so far below.

Logan put out spoons and forks. He folded coarse paper towels under them and sat to wait for dinner. It was getting easier to open his left eye; the shower had helped. His mother stirred sauce into the pasta and carried it to the table. Logan scooped most of the noodles into his pretty blue bowl. He paused when the spoon scraped the bottom and flushed.

"Go ahead, eat up," his mother said. "You're a growing boy and you've got a lot of healing to do."

He reluctantly left only a little food for his mother. Logan's stomach rumbled. He hadn't eaten since breakfast and that seemed an eternity ago. Lynn said a short grace over dinner and Logan dove into his food like a falcon on his prey. His mother picked at her pasta, but ate very little. She was very thin, he thought, but still the prettiest lady on Prianus. She looked worried and Logan hoped she wasn't worrying about him.

Logan couldn't avoid Sullis and his gang for long. They caught up with him a week later, after school. Logan was almost home and felt the first surge of relief at the sight of his building at the end of the street.

"Hey, whore-son!"

He turned just in time to see Sullis charging out from one of the drip-dens. The other people on the sidewalk parted, unwilling to get caught in yet another bout of gang violence. Sullis' eyes were glassy and dilated, his rough cheeks brightly flushed as some chemical coursed through his blood and set his heart racing.

Logan balled his small hands into fists, but remembered his mother's words. As a dozen of Sullis' boys followed their leader out of the murky den and into the crowded street, Logan turned on his heels and ran.

"Where are you off to?" they shouted, chasing Logan and laughing to one another. "Come back! We just want give our best to your mum."

Logan reached the bottom of the stairs. His worn shoes rang on the rusted steel and he flung himself up the steps as quickly as his short legs would carry him. The staircase shuddered beneath him as Sullis and his cronies closed the gap. They were bigger than Logan and much faster. Would his head start be enough?

There was no time. He fell once, caught himself jarringly on his knees and jumped back to his feet, fumbling the keys from his pocket. One of the other boys was so close now that Logan could hear his labored breath sawing away behind him. It wasn't Sullis, but one of his rangier and less chem-addled friends.

Up on the third story, Logan bolted the last few yards and jolted his key into the door. He twisted as hard as he could. Sweat streamed down the back of his neck, cold as ice melt. With a jerk, Logan unlocked the door and ran inside, flinging the door shut behind him. He spun, reaching for the dead-bolt, but the door had already bounced off a large foot thrust through the gap. Logan's pursuer bellowed in pain. "You little bitch! I'm going to rip your skin off!"

The lanky boy lunged through the door and grabbed Logan. Sullis and the rest were close on his tail. They poured through the door and crowded into the small apartment. Someone slammed the door behind them. Sullis stepped forward, grinning at Logan. His lips seemed very thin and very dark.

"So this is where a rental lives." Sullis' words were slurred by drugs. He casually hooked Logan's legs out from under him and cackled when the boy crumpled to the floor. "Not much, is it? But then, that's about what I expect from a cenmark whore."

"She's not…!" Logan started, but Sullis drove a hard-soled boot into his crotch.

"You've got a lot of mouth for a whore-son. Boys, let's make ourselves at home. His mum rents her body easy enough. I doubt she'll mind sharing her place for a while. What's nice around here, Logan?"

Lynn Centra had to work even later than usual. Some drunk had knocked over a toy display, sending bits of broken plastic flying like the shrapnel of a grenade. It had taken an extra hour to collect the shards, once parts of model dinosaurs that were a favorite among those young Prian children whose parents could afford them.

She fished out a few more clattering pieces from under a shelf and swept them into a dustpan. The plastic was molded on one side with a scaly pattern and painted a mottled blues and reds. Lynn emptied the mess into a waste bin.

She wondered if any of it was salvageable. If she could put the pieces back together, the toy dinosaur might make a good present for Logan. It would be his birthday soon and she didn't have any gifts. Lynn sighed and sealed off the garbage bag. Even if she could somehow piece together the broken model, Logan was getting too old for such things. He was growing up so fast.

Finally finished, Lynn turned off the holographics and locked up the store. She ignored the listless catcalls from the whiskery old men lounging outside and hurried to her car. Highwind was no less filthy and dangerous by night, but at least the deep mountain night hid the worst of it away, out of sight.

An Arcadian woman slouched outside the apartment block when Lynn arrived at home. She had pulled her dirty wings around her against the sharp cold. Lynn felt a stab of pity, but then she caught the oily glint of a nanoblade in the alien's hand. She shuddered and decided to park on the other side of the building.

It was almost midnight by the time Lynn wearily pushed open her door and stepped inside. She heard sobbing. Lynn dropped her purse and turned on the lights. Something, everything was wrong.

The apartment was in shambles. All of the pictures had been torn off of the walls, shredded into pieces, and scattered across the floor. Her clothes, too, were strewn across the tiny living room, some ripped or cut, some stained and soiled. The cheap computer was gone from its corner desk and the sofa sliced open. The window was broken and shards of glass littered the worn carpet. Logan's guitar was smashed and lay like a dead pet in the corner of the room.

Lynn heard sobbing. "Logan?" she shrieked.

He was in the kitchen. The cupboards stood open and empty of food. The boy was covered in drying blood. There was a long cut on his temple that seemed to be the source of most of the red, but his lips were puffy and there were dark, terrible-looking bruises on his thin arms and on his bare back. Logan stood at the counter, cradling shards of blue glass in his hands and weeping broken-heartedly over them as he tried to glue them back together. Logan looked up at his mother's approach.

"They broke your plates," he whispered.

"My God," Lynn choked. She batted the broken glass out of his hands and held Logan close. "Oh, my God. Are you alright? Did they hurt you?"

It was a stupid question. Of course they hurt him. Lynn scooped Logan into her arms and carried him out to the car.

She needed to take him to the hospital. As she buckled him into the passenger seat, Logan cried.

"I'm sorry, I'm sorry," he sobbed. "I couldn't stop them!"

"Logan, sweetheart, it doesn't matter. We just need to make sure you're alright."

"They said... and took... I'm sorry." The rest was lost in tears.


"How're you feeling?"

Logan avoided his mother's gaze. He flexed his arms. It was stiff, but not too painful anymore. "Fine," he said. "All better."

"Good."

Lynn patted his shoulder gently and steered him across the hospital lobby, but a young man cleared his throat. "Mrs. Centra?"

She sighed and smiled at Logan. "Why don't you go sit down? I'll come get you in a minute."

Lynn pointed to a row of white plastic chairs, each stamped with the words Property of Highwind Municipal Hospital. Logan nodded and padded across the scarred tile. He sat down beside a middle-aged woman who greeted him limply and then resumed her wet coughing.

Logan watched his mother. She spoke softly to the man behind the desk, quietly so her son couldn't hear. But he knew what they were talking about – money, of course. It was expensive to see doctors on Prianus. Logan heard stories at school about other Alliance planets, closer to the core where there were lots of the silver-skinned Ixthians who all but gave away their medical expertise to anyone, even criminals and the poor. But that was far away. There weren't many Ixthians on Prianus.

Logan kicked his legs. They didn't quite reach the floor. The woman in the next chair smiled, charmed by the ostensibly cute display. But Logan wasn't trying to be cute. He was angry. His blood felt hot in his veins and seemed to burn behind his eyes. His legs were short and thin, knees still raw and red. He was weak, too weak to defend his mother's home and honor. If Logan was going to beat Sullis, he would need help. A lot of help.

His mother was done talking to the receptionist and signed something on a computer screen that Logan was too far away to read. She gestured him over and offered the sullen boy a tight smile.

"Let's go home," she said. "You need your rest."

His mother had already gone to work by the time Logan woke the next morning. The broken cupboards were still empty, but she had left a candy bar and small sleeve of crackers atop a note.

*Love you, my hawk. Have a good day in school.*

Logan stuffed the food into his mouth and left the scrap of paper. He wasn't going to school today. He had more important things to take care of.

The rising sun pierced the thick haze of Highwind sky in silver-gray needles, sharp rays like impossibly slender nanoknives. The streets were busy, as always, full of the thick, noisy bustle.

Though not many Prians could afford NI vehicles, even the air was alive with traffic. Hawks and falcons streaked across the sky and shrieked at one another as their paths crossed or even collided. Feathers – or less pleasant leavings – dropped onto the hats and shoulders of those walking, riding or driving below.

It was full summer, but the thin air remained bitterly cold. Logan cinched his wool coat tightly around him and began his hunt. None of the adults took any notice of the young boy shouldering past. He stopped at the mouth of every alleyway and at the door of every dark bar and smoky drip-den. Heavy-set bouncers turned Logan away from many of these, but most simply ignored him or demanded entry fees, none of which the boy could pay. When he exhausted every place within walking range of his apartment, Logan took a bus deeper into High-wind and continued his search.

He stopped to peer through the window of a worn-looking palaestrum. Inside was a wood-floored gymnasium where a stout balding man was practicing the Prian martial forms. A pair of women in loose-cut clothes studied the short man intently and tried to mimic his movements. Logan caught a reflection in the mirror and turned. A boy about his own age vanished into the dark alley that separated the palaestrum from the shop next door. Logan followed him through the narrow passage and behind the building.

Logan finally found what he was looking for. When he came around the crumbling brick corner, he was suddenly face-to-chest with a tall teenage boy. Behind him, Logan could see the younger one he had followed and seven or eight other boys. A pair of girls, little more than children – much like the boys – lounged against a door and watched as they rubbed runny red noses.

The boy before Logan didn't look anything like Sullis, but he didn't have to. He held himself with the same defensive, suspicious hunch. His breath carried the same reek of cheap rollers. He was exactly the same as Sullis.

"What do you want, you little prick?" he asked Logan.

"I want in. I want to fly with you and your boys."

"You've heard of Elson and my boys, eh? And you want a piece of the cuttings," laughed the boy, who must have been Elson.

"Yes," said Logan simply.

Elson crossed his arms. His jacket had only one sleeve, showing off a sloppy falcon tattoo on the other bared bicep. The ruffian leaned in close to inspect Logan. "You're a bit of a starling, aren't you? Got a piece? A knife or a gun? No? Can't say you're impressing me much, little lark."

Logan didn't back away from the looming boy. "I've got even better. I live across town. There's another gang there, run by a boy called Sullis. Do you know him?"

"No. And why in the sooty hells should I care? This is my patch," said Elson.

"They hit a house not very long ago. They stole some things. Some antiques from Axis. They're really expensive, worth a lot of colour."

The lie sat uneasily in Logan's stomach, as though he had

swallowed a live snake. Sullis had stolen some food and his mother's computer, but had been too stupid to recognize the real prize. He and his boys had smashed all of the pretty dishes one by one as they ignored Logan's pleas to stop. The memory of the shattered blue glass hardened his resolve. Elson's almost colorless brows shot up.

The girls squealed at something and called for Elson's attention, but he waved them off. "You can show us where?" he asked.

"Yes. I know all their favorite places."

"And what do you want, little lark? Just a cut or something else?" Elson asked. He was a little sharper than he looked. He must have guessed that Logan wanted more than a few cen in stolen goods. "Something personal?"

"They said things," replied Logan shortly. "They lied about my mother and ruined her house. I don't want them to ever do it again."

"You want yourself some revenge?"

"Yes."

Elson grinned lazily like a self-satisfied cat. "And that's why you want in. Alright, lark. Let's say what you've got in mind sounds good. Even so, you can't just ask your way into Elson's boys, eh? You've got to prove yourself."

Logan frowned impatiently. "Fine. What do you want me to do?"

Elson gestured to one of his boys. "You got some paint on you? Yeah? Give it here."

The boy plucked a pressure-tube of lumapaint from his

jacket pocket and tossed it to Elson, who held it out to Logan.

"What do you want me to do with it?" Logan took the tube in his small hands, turning it over.

"All this," Elson swept his arms across the alleyway, "is our nesting, isn't it? How about leaving a little reminder for all the other little pricks who want a piece?"

The alley was layered in graffiti, all colors and sizes, from insults to lewd pictures to any number of gang tags. Elson's wasn't the only one to claim this area. Logan hefted the paint and flicked back the cap. He looked up at his new leader.

"My name. Big as you can, lark."

Behind Elson, the girls called out again. The rear door of the palaestrum banged open and a man stomped out into the alley. It was the same short, thick-bellied man Logan had seen inside. Elson turned to face him, forgetting Logan in an instant.

"What do you want, Vorus?" he snapped. "Tail it out of here, you wing-clipped sod."

"You seem to have missed the front door again," the old man answered pleasantly. "You can come in for classes any day, Elson. Why do you insist on vandalizing my back door instead?"

"Not interested," Elson spat. "Go away!"

The gang leader prodded Vorus in his wide chest. With a sad-sounding sigh, Vorus caught Elson's wrist and twisted, driving the tall boy to his knees on the alley floor. "You must learn respect, boy."

Elson shrieked and his gang skittered back like frightened deer. "Let go of me!"

Vorus released the boy, who stumbled back. But instead of running, Elson pulled a snub-nosed laser pistol from his belt and waved it in the air.

"How dare you touch me, you mud-sucking old coot!" he screamed, leveling the gun at Vorus.

The old man lashed out with a surprisingly high, agile kick that cracked against Elson's hand. Elson dropped his laser with a howl and cradled his broken fingers against his chest. He stumbled and ran, scattering his own gang in his haste to escape. The other boys fled down the alleyway, shouting and shrieking. Logan turned to follow, but Vorus grabbed the boy's thin arm.

"No, not you," he said.

"I didn't do anything!" Logan protested.

Vorus looked at the tube of paint in his hand. "You were about to, weren't you?"

Logan dropped the lumapaint, but the old man didn't let him go. Vorus hauled Logan easily through the door and into the palaestrum. They were in a back room, not the one Logan had seen through the front window. There was a square table and a few chairs. Vorus pushed the boy down into one of these. A brown and black falcon perched on a stand under the window and chewing contentedly on his thick braided leash.

"What do you want?" Logan asked petulantly

"What did you think you were doing out there? Why aren't you at school?"

The boy didn't answer.

Vorus sighed and dropped heavily into a chair across the table. He leaned back and rested scarred hands on his belly. "What's your name, little hawk?"

"Logan Centra."

"I heard you talking out there," Vorus said, "about your mother and another boy. Sullis? Is that his name?"

"You were spying on me?" Logan bristled indignantly. He jumped to his feet, but Vorus gave the table a sharp shove. The feet scraped loudly over the bare concrete floor and the edge hit Logan hard in the stomach. He dropped back into his chair, suddenly winded and a little nauseous.

"What did this Sullis kid say that made you come all the way across Highwind to join another gang?" asked Vorus.

"He... he called my mum a whore," Logan panted. "It's a lie! She's not! And then he came to our house and... and broke her things..." He trailed off and looked down at his lap, hoping that Vorus couldn't see the angry tears that stung his eyes.

"He dishonored your mother and your home," Vorus said. He actually sounded as though he agreed. Logan looked up again and found the old man nodding at him. "Tell me, little hawk, why did you want to take Elson and his boys to fight Sullis' gang? Was it out of revenge?"

"I just want Sullis to stop! I want him to leave me and my mother alone! He broke her favorite dishes and sent me to the hospital," said Logan hotly. He had found his breath again. "It was expensive and now mum has to pay for it. It's not fair!"

"This boy, Sullis, is a criminal. What he did was wrong and

against the law."

"I know that!"

"But what about what you were doing? If you defaced my palaestrum, if you joined Elson's gang, you would be a criminal, too."

"But…" Logan protested. Vorus beetled his smooth, shiny brow at the boy.

"No. If you want to fight for honor, you must fight with honor, little hawk. Do you want to learn how?"

"I'm not very good at fighting," replied Logan sullenly.

"No, I can see that," Vorus said, eyes lingering on the boys many bruises. "But you can be, if you work hard, practice every day and come to all of my classes."

"Your classes? Are you any good?"

Vorus laughed and slapped his hand on the table. "Me? Of course I'm good! I'm one of the best. I was a cop for most of my life, Logan. I still teach police and anyone else who wants to fight for the right reasons."

"You think I could be any good?" The idea was tantalizing.

"You need a lot of training. You're small and more than a little skinny, but when Sullis dishonored your mother, you went in search of allies and convinced them to do your work for you," said Vorus. He shook his finger at Logan. "It was very bad idea, but not half clever for a little boy."

"I'm not a little boy!"

"Yes, you are, but I think we can remedy that," Vorus chuckled. His round face became deadly serious. "But I don't teach criminals, little hawk. Do you understand? I train men of honor and integrity. Are you a good man, Logan?"

"Welcome to my palaestrum, Mrs. Centra. I'm Arctan Vorus," he said, extending his hand. "I was hoping we could have a word about Logan."

"You stay the hell away from my son!"

Lynn Centra's face was pale. She was taller than Vorus, but still managed to look small and frightened. Her high heels clacked on the age-scarred wooden floor as she moved to leave.

"Please, Mrs. Centra..." Vorus put a gnarled hand on her shoulder. "Logan needs help."

"Not from you!" Lynn gripped her purse tightly against her knotting stomach. "I don't want you encouraging him, Master Vorus. Please, just leave him alone!"

"Logan's a fighter, Mrs. Centra. He's got fire in his heart and you should count yourself lucky that he's got something to fight for."

Lynn laughed shortly. The sound was sharp and unpleasant, full of bitter pain. "Whether you fight for something or nothing at all, you still end up dead."

"He's shown promise, Mrs. Centra. He's small for his age, but he'll get his growth. Logan's fast and he's clever. I think he has what it takes to be one of the best, maybe even good enough to join the force. Don't you want the best for him?"

"I don't want Logan to be a cop!"

Vorus frowned deeply. "The Prian police are a very thin,

very fragile line between civilization and bloody anarchy here. Prianus needs good men."

"No! I wanted better for Logan. His father was cop, too, and died before he could even hold his son." Lynn was still afraid but her eyes took on the fierce, hard cast of a mother hawk defending her nest. "He left us alone. And for what? Honor?"

"I'm sorry, I didn't know. Logan never mentioned it."

"He doesn't know," Lynn said. She could not meet Vorus' gaze. "I don't want Logan to know. I don't want to lose my son, too."

"I found Logan in the alley out back, trying to join a gang. Is that any better? He wants to fight for you and he'll find a way to do it."

"He sings, you know," answered Lynn quietly. "And plays the guitar. He's amazing, really. I don't know where Logan gets it. Neither his father or I ever played. I always hoped that maybe he would get away from Prianus."

"Maybe he will. Or maybe he'll stay and fight for all of the people who can't or won't fight for themselves. That's not our decision. That's between Logan and God. I just want to teach him. What he does with the knowledge is up to him."

"What if he breaks his hand in your class?"

"Then he'll learn to play his guitar with crooked fingers."

Lynn sighed. "I can't pay for classes, Master Vorus."

"Then I won't charge. He can wash the mirrors and sweep the floors. We'll work it out."

Lynn shook her head, scattering the tears that had gathered in her lashes. Vorus was right, no matter how much she hated it. Slowly, she went to the door and pushed it open. Logan jumped up from where he had been sitting against the wall outside. She brushed the grit from the seat of his pants and took a steadying breath.

"Logan, you can study fighting with Master Vorus. Pay attention and be sure to behave yourself," Lynn said. She smoothed her son's hair and smiled. "I'll see you tonight for dinner, my brave little hawk."

He kissed his mother on the cheek then looked up to see Vorus waiting just inside the palaestrum door. "Are you ready to begin?" the old man asked.

"Yes," Logan answered.

# Amos Was Here

## By Doug Donley

The graffiti crops up across Minneapolis, scrawled on the wall for no obvious reason. "Amos was here." Those with discerning eyes know that the words appear where despair has met hope, where tragedy has met triumph. When something good happens, an act of grace, a truth telling, the words, "Amos was here" often appear. Amos, a phantom, a movement operating under the surface, encouraging the best out of people. In a city prone to despair, "Amos was here" is a beacon reminder that all is not lost. No one is alone. Amos was here. This is the story of one who unwittingly started the movement.

An old man with shaking and wrinkled hands opened the door to his shop the same as he had for fifty years, though today, he slumped under the despondence of his failing health. Today was his last at the shop he had called home.

Like most of us, he took stock of his life and asked the age-old question: Did I make any difference at all? The man's name was Amos. We don't know if it was his real name. We do know that he liked the Biblical story about the unlikely prophet who preached when no one would listen. He took it as his mantle. His moniker.

Amos was a fixture in Minneapolis. He spent time as a preacher, a community organizer, but mostly as a barber. His shop, nestled into a corner just off Nicollet Mall had a trinity of old-school barber chairs. There were several old pews saved from one of the local churches that closed down. Whether you were there for a trim or a warm cup of coffee, you were welcome at Amos' place. On the walls were quotes that he found hopeful.

"We all do better when we all do better."—Paul Wellstone.

"Don't think a small group of people can't change the world. In fact, it is the only thing that ever has"—Margaret Mead.

"Let justice flow down like waters and righteousness like an everflowing stream."—Amos.

"I'd rather collide than collude."—Saul Alinsky.

People would get a trim and then add to the wall. Over the years his walls became a collage of quotes, comics and conversation starters. Only the truly dim or boring could not find something to strike their fancy. It was community art. The words complemented each other, provided contrast, reflected eras and concerns of his clientele. He looked at the walls and tried to remember each instance, each person, each conversation that had been sparked by this or that saying.

He wasn't always a barber. He had wanted to be a missionary tending for the lost souls. But he ran up against the orthodoxy of his day. Like so many others, he wouldn't jump through the ecclesiastical hoops. Back when things like gay marriage became a line in the sand, he took his stand on the side of equality. He advocated for the welcome of everyone to the rites of the church. This marked him as too dangerous for church so he found himself without a job. With a calling, but not a job. He had put himself through school cutting hair—ten bucks in the seminary kitchen for a trim. It was for food money and a couple of beers on a good week. He took the job in the shop out of desperation—besides it was only for a little while—biding his time until the church lightened up or became more welcoming. That was fifty years ago.

"Have a little faith," his former church colleagues said. It was a righteous sounding way of dismissing a concern, no matter how rooted in fact and experience.

*Have a little faith.*

He mused to his clients as they sat in his chair: "We had a little faith that dictators would not do unto others what they didn't want done unto them. We had a little faith that oil companies would clean up their own messes. We had a little faith that banking industries would look out for the small people.

We had a little faith that bigger was better. But as we had that faith we conveniently forgot that the Biblical mandate was to oppose powers and principalities, expose their injustices and restore the streets to living, as the Prophet Isaiah said in the 58th chapter of his book. When we put our faith in a person, a dollar sign, a catch slogan, then we are victims of idolatry. Have a little faith in God. And remember that God is not the oil company, the president, the CEO or even the preacher. God is above all of that and weeps when we abuse each other. The long arc of history bends toward justice and God is the creator of the arc."

He mastered his art of argument, in large part because people would disagree with him and poke holes in his weaker points. He often wondered if he had been a church preacher whether his parishioners would have been so honest. Besides, folks tend to argue much more gently when someone is wielding a sharp object near their jugular.

In his chair sat the shaggy, the high and tight, the bald and in denial. His chair was his own little pulpit, with an individual pew and a captive audience. Some found his chair to be their confessional, knowing that Amos would not judge. They came looking for wisdom, support, companionship and the banter that helped them make it through the day.

As he clipped away at thinning hair, sculpting art out of cranial oddities and bad comb-overs, he would wonder aloud about the state of the world and our own state and stake in such a world. Some came because the need to just talk or to unload, but most just listened. Some even scheduled a ride in his chair every couple of weeks whether or not their hair needed it. They needed his wisdom, his counsel, his perspective.

He was smart. He knew when to say a lot and when to let the silence speak. He knew people came to his place because they liked his stories. They liked his perspective on the world.

There was a time when there were enough jobs to keep shops like his open, when people could buy on credit and not worry about how to pay for it, when things like stadiums were the biggest concerns, but Amos worried. He worried about what would happen when the housing bubble burst, when banks called in their loans, when people took up arms to save their property. And just like he predicted it would, the banks did foreclose, the economy tanked, people got crazy and took it out on each other. Amos advised his grieving clients that they need not be defined by their income, their home, their wealth. He encouraged them to latch onto something more powerful. The barber and clients imagined ways to make a difference in their community, ways to infuse their neighborhood with grace. Think of what a cruel joke it would be to offer hope in the face of such degradation.

He would often quote from the book of Amos as he combed and clipped hair. The book of Amos was written at a time of prosperity when the people of Judah thought that they could do no wrong. The word of God came to Amos and mocked their religious services so big on beauty, but devoid of any real meaning beyond the doors. He quoted from the 5th chapter: "I hate, I despise your festivals and I take no delight in your solemn assemblies. Take away from me the noise of your songs; I will not listen to the melody of your harps. But let justice flow down like waters and righteousness like an ever-flowing stream." He encouraged people to do simple acts of justice. Simple acts of mercy, acts of compassion. It's the only thing that stops the evil. He looked at the quote from Martin Luther King "Love is more powerful than hate."

This caught the imagination of one of his customers. He left a wad of cash in the door of an immigrant family's home, which was soon to be foreclosed. The contribution was anonymous, except for a little note that said "Amos was here." He told the barber his story, but swore him to secrecy. But secrets have a way of getting out and pretty soon others were copying the acts of goodness and charity. Each was anonymous except for the tag line, "Amos was here." They would then come back and whisper that Amos had shown up. They laughed about it in the barber chair. Amos could almost hear their voices, the conspiratorial joy that came from doing something unexpected and even good.

He noticed another quote. This one he wrote himself in a particularly dark moment:

"Faith isn't doing great things. Faith is getting up everyday and doing something. Sometimes the most profound thing is the most mundane." That's how he saw his work. Cut the hair, speak the truth, try to not get sucked down into the vortex of despondency. He got comfort from his people and the stories they shared. He lived vicariously through them. Each quote on the wall was a witness to what they shared, what they hoped for, what they imagined. He knew full well that a prophet is lonely only when no one listens. Unlike the Amos of scripture, this Amos had faithful companions. Religion has been used to placate the masses, numbing them to the workings of the empire of the hour. But in Amos' chair people imagined a different reality.

He encouraged people to imagine a better future. And he reminded them that the only way to ensure that was to create a better present. Folks shared the stories of when they protested in the streets, sometimes all by themselves, sometimes surrounded by a critical mass that demanded attention—making them the darling of the evening news feed—something to keep people's minds occupied.

When the cataclysm of 2037 hit, many were shocked—everyone that is except for those who remembered their history. The story is as old as the biblical narrative. As soon as the Hebrew people grew comfortable with their temple and land, others would seek to take it away. In order to keep it, they made sweeping generalizations about outsiders, saw them as a threat, and lost their sense of generosity and welcome. In the end their temple was destroyed and they were sent into exile, just as their prophets had predicted. Centuries later, a prophet named Jesus reiterated the words of the most radical of the ancient prophets and for all of his good works he was executed by the state in cahoots with organized religion that tried to keep the peace at all costs. Of course, it didn't work. You can silence a person, but not a movement.

The same scenario has been playing out for centuries. And each year, a lonely prophet emerges, tells the truth and is at first ignored, then laughed at, then fought against. In retrospect, the prophet is hailed as an insightful leader. When their dire predictions about the corporate greed, the military industrial complex, and the religion that gave it divine sanction came true, which they almost always did, the people wondered how they could be so blind. But not so with the people who occupied Amos' chair. At one point, Amos wrote on the wall, "In order to win a war, one must convince people that they are fighting a holy war. But, you must never see yourself as accountable to God"—Machiavelli.

Now, as Amos cleaned out his shop for the last time, he studied the walls again and wondered if anything he had done had been worth it. Five decades of rabble-rousing, community organizing, clipping and preaching. He needed to make way for someone younger, quicker on the uptake, better able to navigate the changing landscape—someone who wasn't dying.

He remembered Minneapolis back in the Day. He looked at the collage on the wall and remembered the days when people argued about where to put stadiums while shifting the blame for any hardship onto the backs of the poor. He remembered backroom deals where politicians gave bailouts to their funders and their friends. Who would stand for the poor? Who would stand for the outcast? Like his Biblical namesake, he spoke when no one else seemed to be listening. He spoke ancient language of love and acceptance and equality and justice.

Making things fair and fighting against those too selfish is the job of a person of faith. If that makes him or her a laughing-stock, so be it.

"What gives you life?" He saw that one on the wall. It remind-ed him of smug customers who talked about things they had, the collection of goodies that left no lasting mark. He gently won-dered aloud to his customers "what about you gives someone else life?" He challenged those who made God in their own image—their own personal piggy bank, cheering section, bailer-outer.

He had a list of things on the wall that no longer existed: the slide rule, the Atari Computer, the VCR, the mailbox, the in-ternal combustion engine, the option to ignore your neighbor.

What the barber didn't realize was the number of people that he had influenced. He didn't know about the movements he had spawned. He didn't recognize the impact he had on people's lives.

One day, Amos walked into the convenient store down the street. A man was berating a woman, calling her names, in-sulting her. With each insult he hurled at her, she shuddered slightly more. She knew eventually a blow would punctuate his words. She survived merely through endurance and a vague hope that he'd lose steam. This time he chose to let loose pub-licly. Most people looked the other way. No one knew if he would draw a gun or a knife. No one wanted to be in the cross-fire. No one that is, but Amos. He walked up to the man and positioned himself nearby the woman. He looked in his eyes and said, "I'm just going to stand here." He didn't say, "Stop".

Amos didn't point out that that the man was making a fool of himself—that was obvious. But he did acknowledge that others noticed his abusive behavior and it would not go unchecked. Not this time. The man backed down and the woman demurely nodded a thank you. Amos later preached a sermon about it from his perch behind his barber chair. A client wrote the words on the wall: "Don't just do something, stand there."

"We are all witnesses to injustice and violence," Amos would say. "Our role is to divert it and imagine a new way of being for the community. Don't just do something, stand there."

He used humor to diffuse situations, taught people that there was a better way to address grievances than by violence.

Sometimes, it's true he was as cynical as the next person. His humor was spiteful. He was quick to insult and demonize. He listened to radio that fed his cynicism and never challenged his worldview. In his lower moments, he didn't believe anything could get any better. It was what you might call a crisis of faith. But that's also when he leaned the most on the people in his chair. They reminded him of hope, even when he forgot about it. They whispered about the places where they had scratched the words, "Amos was here."

That's one of the things that drew people to him. He was honest and never satisfied with a platitude.

When the riots took place, he opened his door not only to cut hair, but also to offer sanctuary.

Whatever happens, a barbershop is a constant. That's one thing you can't do virtually or by yourself (unless you want to look like an idiot). He had a sign above his chair that said, "The one who cuts his own hair has a fool for a barber." It was the ultimate in job security. He gave children their first haircuts and old men their last ones. Students relied on him to make them look cool and keep up with the latest follicle fad.

He knew how to plant a seed. He told the story of Shiprah and Puah from the book of Exodus. They were the Egyptian midwives who refused to kill the Hebrew male babies on the birth stool. Shiphrah and Puah told Pharoah, "Gee, each time we get there, the baby's already born. The Hebrew women are too strong for us." They were responsible for the protected births of hundreds of Hebrew children—children who would eventually demand to be set free from Egypt. Their act of civil disobedience ensured the birth of Moses and a generation that would lead the Hebrew people out of slavery. He said it to the most discouraged person in the shop, but the one who also had the tools to be a good community organizer, "I wonder if there are Shiprhahs and Puahs out there."

It came as no surprise, then, when that awkward guy formed the Shiphrah and Puah Society (SAPS). The Shiphrah and Puah Society saw as their calling to be the midwives of a revolutionary movement. They were to shelter subversive movements, teach them the ways of resistance, and empower them to make changes in the world. He wrote on the wall, "Most revolutions are inspired either by Revelation or by Exodus. It's either the liberation from slavery or the destruction of all humanity."

Now Amos was looking over the tapestry of his shop. Reflecting on the mementos of his career, he contemplated what it would have been like had he traded this simple truth-telling life for a more lucrative one. One where he made friends and influenced people.

He could have had the nice house in the suburbs—back when there were suburbs. He could have had the American Dream—back when there was an American Dream—but every time he tried it, something pulled him back—or made him self-destruct. It was push-pull. In retrospect he saw it as a Divine hand slapping him down, or waking him up to his real role. That's why he took on the name of Amos, the truth-telling prophet who showed people a better way. It suited him.

As the coffee brewed, he took down an old picture of himself as a young man. He was standing on a street corner with his fist in the air, a laugh on his face and a sign around his neck that read, "Amos was here." On the one blank wall where the picture had hung, he added one last quote to the wall, as an epitaph.

"What if?

What if? That's the question that lingers on the tips of our tongues.

What if we saw this coming?

What if we knew global warming was going to send us down this spiral of environmental degradation? Who knew that we would prefer the convenient lie to the inconvenient truth?

What if we did not support dictators so that we could have a monopoly on wealth in the world?

What if we saw the long-term consequences of trickle-down economics?

What if we embraced the statement Paul Wellstone made famous: "We all do better when we all do better"?

What if we only believed in higher power that could restore us to sanity? The first step is to admit that we are sick. What if we admitted just such a thing?

What if we took the lessons of 9-11 and chose to actually be a more compassionate people?

What if we stopped polluting our Minnesota rivers so that there was not a dead zone 2000 miles downstream?

What if we did justice, loved mercy and walked humbly with God as the Prophet Micah suggested?

The prophets of old wondered the same thing. What if? What if?

What if we truly believed? Not just in God.

What if we believed that there was a better way?

What if we embraced the things that seem like such common sense when looked at in retrospect.

What if we cared as much about each other as we do about ourselves?

I wonder, what if we saw beauty with a wider eye?

What if we took up our mantle and helped someone else?

What if we did not take no for an answer?

What if we planted seeds of subversion?

What if we made our presence known?

What if we are the ones for whom we have been waiting?"

He finished the coffee and turned off the pot. He fiddled with the keys, and then thought against it. He left the door open wondering, hoping, knowing that the art on the wall or its descendants would reach other hands and hearts.

Picture under his arm, Amos walked down the street, a phantom dissolving into the crowd.

The End

# About The
# Authors

# John Beckmann

## Author of
*Zombielzebub:*
*Hell's Invasion*

John Beckmann is a Twin Cities based printmaking artist. He grew up and went to high school in Farbault, Minnesota where he played football and swam. Later he attended college and graduated Summa Cum Laude from the University of Minnesota (2009) with dual Bachelors degrees in Physiology and Art.

Currently John is studying to receive his PhD in Entomology. His research focuses on the molecular interactions between mosquitoes and an obligate intracellular organisms, Wolbachia: which itself lives in the testes and ovaries of the Mosquitoes.

John Lives in Minneapolis with his wife, Shawna, daughter, Jane, and Newfoundlands, Helga and Odin. He enjoys making art, music, bugs, mosquitoes, diseases (at least learning about them), and beer brewing.

## Websites
Website: http://www.stampedepress.com
Facebook: https://www.facebook.com/stampedepress
Twitter: http://www.twitter.com/stampedepress

# Doug Donley

## Author of
*Amos Was Here*

Doug Donley is a native of Cleveland, Ohio and has lived in New York City, Hartford, Connecticut, and San Francisco, California before settling in the Twin Cities in 2001. Most of his writing takes place at University Baptist Church where he serves as pastor. He lives in Mounds View with his wife and two daughters.

In his spare time, he chauffeurs his kids to various events, runs marathons, and engages the neighborhood in making backyard maple syrup. An activist, he has been to Nicaragua eight times and serves on the Board of the Baptist Peace Fellowship of North America, the Minnesota Religious Coalition for Reproductive Choice and chairs the U of M's Interfaith Campus Coalition.

## Websites
Writings: http://www.ubcmn.org/

# Brian D. Garrity
## Author of
*Bullseye, Inc.*

Growing up in western Wisconsin, Brian D. Garrity spent much of it living on the Mississippi River. After moving to the Twin Cities to attend the Minneapolis College of Art and Design, he became entrenched in the local underground art and music scene.

During the nineties and beyond, Brian was a photographer, shooting bands for national and international music magazinzines.

In 2005, he self-published the novella, Ready-Made Dreams, and Onyx Neon Press included the dystopian short Godless in their 2010 Sci-Fi anthology, *Cifiscape Vol. I, The Twin Cities. Still Waters Run Deep*, a Novel chronicling the misadventures of River Rats on the upper Mississippi during the 70's, was self published in the Fall of 2010, and is available at Amazon.com. Brian currently resides in Minneapolis, in a nearly continuous state of astonishment.

## Websites
Website: http://www.briangarrity.com

## Other Work by Brian D. Garrity
*Still Waters Run Deep* available on Amazon

# Jonathan Hansen

## Author of
*Harris*

Jonathan Hansen has worked behind counters, entered data, managed restaurants and run the booth at mutliplex theatres. He's been on-line tech support, a site manager for film and TV shoots and a service coordinator at a cemetery older than Los Angeles and set smack dab in the middle of Hollywood.

He is now living in Minneapolis with his wife and two spoiled cats, writing short stories and querying agents about his first book, Gunslingers of the Apocalypse -- a two-fisted adventure set in a world overrun by zombies -- while deciding on his next project.

Websites
Twitter: http://twitter.com/hansen_sogroovy
Blog: http://jon-this-is-mine.blogspot.com

# Max Hrabal

## Author of
*The Man with Two*
*Hearts in His Ribcage*

Max Hrabal was born in St. Paul and grew up in Minneapolis where he attended public schools and played on park sports teams.

Eventually he went to college on the west coast and has since worked at various jobs and spent some time in a few other countries. He is a teacher now and calls Minnesota home.

# Bob Lipski

## Author of
### *The Fall Of The World's Own Optimist*

Bob Lipski has been making comics for ten years now with the comic book *Uptown Girl* as his most recognized work.

His next book, *Little Adventures* will be out in 2012. He lives in Saint Paul, Minnesota with his wife Amy and their two children, Ryan and Sophie. He also has a one-eyed dog named Ernie, and a cat he is fairly indifferent to.

## Websites
Website: http://www.uptowngirlcomic.com
Blog: http://boblipski.wordpress.com

## Other Work by Bob Lipski
*Uptown Girl Vols. 1-6* available on Amazon

# Erica Lindquist
# & Aron Christensen
# Authors of
## *Little Hawk*

Erica Lindquist writes science fiction and fantasy novels with her husband, Aron Christensen. They have no formal training in writing, but that's never stopped them.

Their work includes the *Reforged Trilogy*, *In the House of Five Dragons* and *The Dead Beat*.

## Websites
Twitter: http://twitter.com/LLStories
Blog: http://looseleafstories.com

## Other Work by Erica & Aron
*Reforged, Book 1: Anvil of Tears* - available on Amazon

*Reforged, Book 2: Sword of Dreams* - available on Amazon

*In the House of Five Dragons* available on Amazon

*The Dead Beat Vol. I* available on Amazon

# Dale Newton
## Author of
*Wardrobe Malfunctions*

By day, he's an ordinary government communicator who has cranked out scores of news releases, brochures, fact sheets, public service announcements, and video scripts. By night (and weekends), he indulges his other interests. Dale Newton has co-authored three books on independent filmmaking, and he has written magazine articles, a half-dozen screen plays, and several stage plays. He's the writer and producer of the feature-length science fiction movie, *Resident Alien*.

He resides in a household on the Minnesota side of the St. Croix River where he has the only "Y" chromosomes.

## Websites
Website: http://newtonsbrain.wordpress.com

## Other Work by Dale Newton
*Persistence of Vision: An Impractical Guide to Producing a Feature Film for Under $30,000* available on Amazon

*Digital Filmmaking 101: An Essential Guide to Producing Low-Budget Movies* available on Amazon

*Top 10 Reasons Why It's a Great Time to be a Filmmaker* available on Amazon

# David Oppegaard

## Author of
### *The Rotations of the Earth*

David Oppegaard is the Bram Stoker-nominated author of *The Suicide Collectors* and *Wormwood, Nevada*.

A resident of St. Paul, MN, David co-hosts a comedic film review podcast called *When Harry Met Fatty* and teaches a slipstream fiction course at The Loft Literary Center.

## Websites
Website: http://www.davidoppegaard.com
Twitter: http://www.twitter.com//DavidOppegaard

## Other Work by David Oppegaard
*The Suicide Collectors* available on Amazon

*Wormwood, Nevada* available on Amazon

# Aaron M. Wilson

## Author of
*Lethal Options*

Aaron M. Wilson is a full-time dad who lives in Minneapolis. He is the author of The Many Lives of Inez Wick, a collection of short fiction that follows Inez as she fights polluters and those who would spoil the natural world. He is also a frequent short story contributor to eFiction Magazine.

## Websites
Twitter: http://twitter.com/SoullessMachine
Blog: http://www.soullessmachine.com

## Other Work by Aaron M. Wilson
*The Many Lives of Inez Wick* available on Amazon.com and Lulu

*The Skin Scholarship* available on Lulu

For more information on
the authors or to keep up with
Cifiscape visit
cifiscape.onyxneon.com

Other titles by Onyx Neon Press

# *Gigapolis*
by S. Christopher

# *Gravitas*
by S. Christopher

# *Cifiscape Vol. I, The Twin Cities*
by Ken Avidor, Brian D. Garrity, Toianna Gump, Max Hrabal, Bob Lipski, Ken Lubold, and Aaron M. Wilson.